Andre Gonzalez

Followed Home

Contents

Dedication

This book is dedicated to my grandmothers, Tonie and Esther. Thank you for teaching me so much. You never know who your real heroes are until they are gone.

1

Kyle Wells moaned as snow swallowed him up to his neck. *This snow is insane!* he thought as he returned from his Dad's truck to fetch an extra box of cereal for breakfast. The snow piled up as high as the doorknob, which stood at about chest level, and he had to wriggle his way through the path he had made on his way out. With his scrawny frame, he didn't find it as difficult returning.

When he reached the door, he shook the clinging snow free. A pile of snow had already fallen into the cabin when he opened the door, and he could see the dent that had collapsed in the wall of powder that clung on to the cabin's wooden exterior.

He opened the door to find his father, Travis, sweeping the melting snow off the floor of the cabin entryway. The fireplace crackled behind him in the living room as a deer head watched them from its place above the mantle. The welcome mat had soaked up most of the snow, turning it into a shade of dark red, which reminded Kyle of blood.

"Well, this is a real shit storm, eh?" Travis said. Being the travel day back home, he wore his favorite outfit of sweatpants and a long sleeve tee. He had caught some sun the day before the blizzard hit, leaving his tone a light shade of pink. His dark hair was spiked in the front, a nod to his clinging on of his youth despite being a father to a teenager.

"No shit," Kyle agreed. The boys enjoyed the fact that Travis couldn't care less if they cursed or not while their mothers weren't around. He remembered using every curse word in middle school, when he was away from his parents.

"You're lucky your Mom isn't here. She'd kick your ass if she saw all this snow inside," Travis uttered, happy he had the authority while his wife wasn't around. The boys were almost as tall as him anyway. Kids these days seemed to grow at disgusting rates, in his opinion, but perhaps he was just bitter at never experiencing such a growth spurt.

Kyle kicked off his boots and sat at the kitchen table to enjoy a bowl of the cereal he had worked so hard to get from the truck. His long, curly hair draped over his eyes in waves of brown, hiding his typical groggy complexion after a short night's sleep. His friend, Mikey, sat across the table with his laptop open, pounding away at his keyboard.

Mikey had more brains than anyone in his group of friends and they often wondered why he even hung out with them. He had worked on cutting back his use of big words when he was around them, as they would all look at him like he had spoken Mandarin. Kids at school called him the "Wiz" because he had the answer to everything. He had even built his laptop from scratch. "I just YouTubed it. It wasn't hard," he told his friends when they had gawked at his creation in disbelief.

Kyle believed Mikey would be the first black person to walk on the moon, and he would probably build his own spaceship to get there. He often told Mikey to not "dumb it down" when they were hanging out. Typically, the brains of a class would have minimal friends, or be picked on for being a "nerd", but not Mikey. Every day he felt blessed to have met these friends who empowered him to use his talents while helping him to live a normal teenage life. Sometimes, they had to pull him away from his computer or books to go and throw a football around. Somehow, they even convinced him to join the basketball team, and the coach agreed to let him track stats to help improve the team.

"Listen to this!" Mikey barked in excitement. "I just read an article on 9news that some guy in Denver saw a gray man snooping around his house last night. I swear, the legalization of marijuana is turning people into nutjobs in our city. What a crock!"

"Riiight," Travis replied. "Slow news day I take it."

"Even worse, the guy said it happened at night," Mikey continued, the glare of the screen reflecting off his widened eyes. "If you saw someone outside your house at night, how would you know they had gray skin?"

"Gray people?" Kyle questioned. "Sounds like nonsense to me."

"Ugh, I know. Journalists these days are garbage. They'll literally write anything," Mikey said. "That's why I write my own blogs."

Stomping boots approached the door, likely in order to remove the snow that covered them. "Maybe it's the gray man," Kyle mocked, as his Dad chuckled.

After the rattle of the doorknob, the door swung open, blowing another gust of snow inside.

"Jesus Christ, you kids! I'm glad this is our last day," Travis cried.

"I'm sorry guys!" James Jensen announced, throwing his arms in the air in disgust.

"Nice one, dipshit," said Kyle, laughing.

James -or Jimmy as he preferred to be called- balanced out

Mikey in every sense. He couldn't stand books or studying. All he cared about was playing sports. With an athletic build and a lofty height, he would likely finish high school at a height of more than six feet. Despite his awkward size, he moved quickly and gracefully. He shined in every sports team he played on and the girls loved him. His blonde hair flowed wildly, and his pearly teeth shined when he grinned. His path to fame as the sexy, dumb jock in high school was all but set in stone.

"Relax dudes, I'll clean this mess up," Jimmy declared. He threw his Denver Nuggets beanie onto the ground, causing some left over snowflakes to dust his hair. "Brian isn't back yet?"

"No, I thought he'd left with you this morning?" Kyle asked with a curious look. Jimmy and Brian had gone out into the snow, wanting to be adventurous with the blizzard that made history.

"Yeah, he did, but he wanted to head back here before me," Jimmy explained. "He said he was hungry and wanted to eat."

Kyle felt the stress start to boil inside. They had all visited the cabin at least forty times since they had met in the sixth grade, and everyone knew the area well, even in the midst of a snow-storm.

"I think we might have a problem," Jimmy said, a shadow of fear creeping over his face. "I heard a scream. I thought it was down by the Tucker's cabin, so I didn't think anything of it." The Tuckers neighbored the Wells' cabin about a mile away.

Travis shot up from his lying down position on the couch in the living room. "Jimmy, are you being serious?"

"Yeah, I wouldn't joke about something like this."

"Dad, we need to go find him!" Kyle jumped up from his seat, letting his spoon clang in the empty bowl of cereal.

4

"Absolutely, let's go!" Travis grabbed some more layers of clothing to wear out into the cold. Jimmy and Mikey followed.

Kyle stormed into his room, snagged his hunting rifle, and returned dressed, all in what seemed like a handful of seconds.

"What's that for?" Mikey questioned.

"Well, Jimmy said there was a scream. What if someone is out there?" said Kyle as he loaded the rifle.

"That's not reasonable, Ky." Travis was now fully bundled and ready to begin the search. "We know the Tucker's place is empty this weekend, and there's four feet of snow. There's no way someone is wandering the woods in the middle of nowhere today!"

"He's right, Kyle," Jimmy chimed in, now also ready to go. "Brian's probably fine. I would've seen someone, don'tcha think?"

They all huddled in the living room while Kyle returned the rifle to its safe.

"Okay, let's split up, Travis commanded. "I'll take north towards the Tuckers, Kyle, you go east back towards the main road. Jim and Mike, you head the opposite way, and spread out. If you find him, shout as loud as you can and we'll come."

Mikey slid on his ski goggles as they barged out of the cabin to find Brian. They all shouted his name a couple of times as they broke into their different directions. The shouting died down in disappointment as they reached the conclusion that Brian either could not hear or could not respond.

Kyle headed towards the main road that twisted down from I-70 as his Dad instructed. Having already fought through the snow earlier, he continued the shuffling motion with his feet that he had found to work so well.

He was now out of sight from the cabin, which caused him

5

some anxiety as he looked back and saw nothing but a whiteout of snow that swallowed tons of towering pine trees. Thanks to the whistling wind and the lengthy distance from the cabin, he knew a shout from this distance would never reach the others. Alone in nature, the silence was deafening in his mind. He began to hum as he treaded along some of the pine trees to try and distract his mind. A faint groaning sound like someone makes while they are asleep escaped the trees, chilling Kyle's blood.

"Brian?" Kyle trembled, panicking in his mind.

"Ky!" It was definitely Brian's voice.

"Where are you?" Kyle shouted into the blindness of the storm. Brian's voice seemed to bounce off the trees from every angle.

"Tree...with heart on it," Brian gasped. Clearly he could hardly speak.

Kyle spun around frantically and identified the tree stump that some young lovers must have carved out years ago; a large heart encompassing the chiseled script of *A + N*.

Kyle darted towards the tree, hugging it as he rotated himself around the trunk.

"Holy fuck," Kyle whispered to himself. His knees locked at the sight of a dark red trail, which led to a pool of blood surrounding Brian who lay on the ground with an apparent gash in his leg.

Kyle collapsed to his knees, his whole body tense beyond belief. He forced himself to crawl along the trail of blood towards Brian.

As he approached, Kyle vomited in the snow. Brian's left leg was completely torn open at the thigh. He thought if the flaps of skin were pulled apart any further he would see the femur.

"Wh-what happened?" Kyle asked.

Brian had relaxed somewhat thanks to Kyle's presence and could now speak and breathe a little more clearly. "All I remember...was being sucker punched from behind. Then I woke up with my leg throbbing." Brian paused and glanced around as best he could from his stiff position in the snow.

Kyle peered around, hoping not to see some creep wandering around the woods while his father and friends were nowhere to be seen. He dropped his head back towards the snow, letting the realization of what had just transpired sink in. He gathered his strength and pulled himself back up to his feet. His heart dropped straight into his stomach as he saw a man staring right back at him from between a couple of trees roughly twenty feet away.

The man stood tall, bigger even than Jimmy. He wore baggy snow gear and donned a ski mask, which covered his entire face.

Once the tightening in Kyle's throat let up, he was able to muster a confident, "Who are you?"

His palms were sweating despite the 20 degree weather. The man's ski mask crinkled in the mouth region, leaving Kyle to believe a smile had formed behind the mask. "I'm your worst nightmare, kid," a calm, baritone voice said.

Kyle wished he had his rifle right now. He should have trusted his intuition. He stood there completely defenseless, face to face with a clearly dangerous man twice his size.

"Did you do this?" Kyle questioned.

Nothing but a blank stare out of emotionless snow goggles responded. The man raised his hands to reveal two yellow ski gloves covered in blood, causing Kyle's stomach to twist into tighter knots.

"Look kid," the man said, breaking the silence. "I have some things to do, but I'll see you around."

The man turned and ran back into the thick stand of trees.

"What the fuck?" Brian cried from the ground.

"We need to go to the cabin, get everyone, and leave right away," Kyle cried. "Will you be able to get back on one leg using me as your crutch?"

"I don't have much choice right now." Brian groaned in pain.

Kyle examined the wound, but had no clue on what he could do to help, so he slouched down to wrap Brian around his upper body, and pulled him up as Brian flailed around in an effort to get proper footing on his good leg. He was fortunate to be in the cold, as his entire body had gone numb, making his pain only a soft throb for the moment.

A depressing gray continued to rule the sky, and the falling snow picked up speed again on their way back to the cabin. Kyle and Brian walked in unison, pacing each other's steps through the woods. Brian didn't worry about the man as he could only concentrate on his bleeding leg. Kyle, however, kept looking back to make sure the monster in the ski mask wasn't following them. They were 100 yards away from the cabin, but the snow and paranoia made it feel like 300. He had never seen a soul on his family's property before and couldn't figure out who it might be.

* * * * *

Kyle kicked in the door to the cabin, still half-hugging Brian around the waist. The ritual of snow falling inside continued, but it didn't seem such a big issue this time around. A deserted cabin greeted them. Everyone had left in a panic, yet the fireplace still cracked its soothing tune. The two tumbled into the living room. Brian all but dove onto the couch.

Kyle raced back out of the open door and shouted as loud as he could. "I FOUND HIM! WE'RE AT THE CABIN!"

He ran back inside, slamming the door behind him, and tended to Brian who clenched his leg as he lay on the couch.

Brian's composure surprised him. He was never one to handle adversity with such grace, but something about him seemed more confident than normal.

"I'm still numb, but it'll get warm and wear off. Do we have painkillers?"

"We should," Kyle dashed to the kitchen and rummaged through a cupboard which contained all kinds of medications. "Got it!"

All they had was a mild painkiller and a bandage, but that would have to do for the time being. Brian extended his hand for the pills as Kyle moved towards him with a glass of water. He took four of them and lay back as Kyle wrapped his leg with the bandage.

Kyle felt nauseous as the white bandage instantly changed into a dark red color as it absorbed Brian's blood.

Tears rolled down his cheek as he imagined this devilish man in the ski mask telling him he would "see him around". Kyle wiped away the tears as multiple footsteps paraded toward the front door.

Travis burst into the cabin, panting, followed by Mikey and Jimmy.

"Oh my God," Travis whispered as his eyes met the massacre that had occurred on Brian's leg.

Mikey and Jimmy stood there speechless and both turned pale as they too saw the bloody scene.

"He's losing blood. We need to wrap something tight around his leg," Travis said and grabbed a belt hanging on one of the chairs, fastening it firmly around the bandage. Brian fainted in his already sleeping position. "Tell me what happened."

Kyle explained everything he saw and experienced from the moment he found Brian lying on the ground. The mood in the room stiffened when he spoke of the large man roaming in the woods, and the blood on his gloves.

"We need to leave right now," Travis declared. He always did well at keeping calm in desperate moments. "Everyone pack your bags quickly. We need to get Brian to the hospital. There's no time to wait for an ambulance."

Travis smacked his hands together twice in rapid motion. "Now!"

The boys snapped out of their shock and retreated to their rooms to gather their belongings. It only took five minutes for everyone to throw their belongings into duffel bags and reconvene in the living room. Travis had put out the fireplace before pulling his Dodge pickup right to the front door and was already loading the bags into the bed of the truck.

"Alright, I need two in the front with me. Brian will be laid on the backseat, and the other one of you will need to squeeze in on the floor below him," Travis instructed.

Travis, Kyle, and Jimmy carried the now unconscious Brian into the backseat while Mikey loaded the rest of the bags into the bed. Everything was ready to go and the boys all jammed uncomfortably into the truck.

Travis scraped away inches of snow that had blanketed the windshield. Kyle and Jimmy sat in the front as they stared at the blank white slowly give way to the world as the back and forth motion of the ice scraper glided across the windshield.

Travis hastened into the truck, breathing hard with a dazed look in his eyes.

"Everything okay?" Kyle questioned.

"Yes, we just need to get out of here. It's going to take a long fucking time with these roads," Travis replied in a monotone fashion. He threw the truck into *drive* and headed back towards the main road.

* * * * *

A long fucking time couldn't be closer to the truth. Travis squeezed tight on the steering wheel like he wanted to suffocate it. He had lived in Colorado his whole life and had never seen or driven in snow like this.

Should have gotten those god damned snow tires, he thought as he peered down at the speedometer daring him to accelerate above 20 miles per hour. He had already fishtailed a couple of times.

They crawled down the side road that twisted its way back into the city of Golden. Three feet of hard-packed snow and ice, wind gusts up to 60 miles per hour, and low tread tires hanging on for dear life kept Travis plenty occupied. *If I could just see, this wouldn't be so bad.*

Travis checked the clock on his stereo as it taunted him with a time of 3 p.m. The boys grew restless while Brian kept coming in and out of consciousness. When awake, he gladly contributed to the ongoing argument regarding the hottest girl in their eighth grade class. Brian voted for Monica Duhamel, his life-long crush since the first grade. Even in his weary state of mind, he defended her honor.

Travis couldn't care less and turned his attention to the steady back-and-forth gliding of the windshield wipers dancing across his line of vision. The sky remained an unforgiving gray and dumped more snow, leaving visibility no more than 15 feet on the already treacherous drive back into the city.

Mental fatigue drowned the boys from the events that had transpired earlier in the morning, and they all fell victim to sleep, leaving Travis to drive in silence.

The helpless father let his mind wander as he stared out into the whiteness swirling in every direction. He wished the trip didn't have to end so abruptly. Back home nothing but problems awaited. His marriage was on shaky ground and hiding it from Kyle was mentally exhausting him. Sleeping on the floor in his own bedroom in order to keep the secret, broke every level of his pride. This incident with the friend of Kyle would be sure to spark an instant fight. He could only hope that he would not need to duck flying objects.

As much as he wanted to mentally prepare for the impending fight, he had to keep an intense focus on the road. The snowfall refused to let up and Travis fought his mind from jumping to other thoughts. Visibility vanished before his eyes, and the road conditions worsened by the minute. *It's going to take six fucking hours just to get to Golden.* The headlights only reflected the snow making it look like more than there actually was.

A figure appeared in the road a few feet ahead, which reminded Travis of the movie poster for *The Exorcist*. A dark figure of a man wearing a fedora stood out from the showering of snow. A thick coat slung over the figure and it appeared the man was looking down at the ground, not acknowledging the approaching truck.

He slammed on the brakes and squealed, losing control of the truck as it screeched and slid out of control like a child ice skating for the first time. The headlights revealed the person did indeed have their focus on the ground. The fedora was angled enough to cover the eyes so Travis couldn't get a clean look. The body grew bigger and closer as the truck slid towards it and struck the person straight on, causing their head to violently snap backwards. The dark figure flew back from its standing position into a sprawled out form and slid across the road until it met the stump of a tree roughly 30 feet away. The way the body slid reminded Travis of the stones used in curling during the Winter Olympics.

He threw a glance over his shoulder to find more disaster. Brian had fallen into the space between the front and back seats where Mikey sat. His shredded leg smashed down on Mikey and became pinched underneath a couple of duffel bags that flew forward from behind the head rests. Blood flowed like a river out of the belted down bandage that had turned as black as night.

Brian took one glance down at his leg and fainted again, leaving all his dead weight to crush his helpless friend.

"Is everyone okay?" Travis could barely speak out of his tensed throat.

Kyle gave a steady nod, enough to confirm no harm was done. The shock on his face, however, told another story. Jimmy did the same and looked behind him to see the avalanche of friends in the back. The truck slid to a complete stop and Travis could see the body a few yards ahead, not moving.

"I need you two to get Brian off of Mikey and wake him up," Travis commanded with a crack in his voice, while Mikey grunted from beneath to try and lift his passed out friend himself. "Get his leg re-wrapped as best you can."

Travis flailed at the door handle multiple times before grabbing hold. His hands shook uncontrollably like a severe case of Parkinson's disease. His mind tumbled in its processing of what exactly had just happened. Who in Christ's name had been standing in the middle of the road in this blizzard?

Nothing about this situation made any sense in Travis's flustered brain, but it finally clicked that he had just hit someone with his truck. Although his speed wouldn't exactly win the Indy, it could still have caused some serious problems, or worse.

Unaware of his heightened adrenaline, Travis rammed his shoulder into the door so hard that he shot out of the truck hands-first, diving like a swimmer jumping into a pool of snow. The shock of the situation had numbed his body so he wouldn't feel the gashes on his leg until much later that night.

Once he had gathered himself, he skirted to the front of the truck expecting to see blood and limbs on the snow like freshly butchered meat atop dry ice.

Nothing? Travis couldn't believe his eyes. He *refused* to believe them for that matter. He crouched to get a view below the undercarriage of the truck, hoping he would see *something* to confirm his own sanity.

Nothing there either? Okay. Good, but not really. *I know I saw something, right?* His mind raced out of control. *There's no way I made this up. I saw a person and I hit that person. Hard.*

He glared back down at the spot of impact where he had hit the body. Tire tracks illustrated the path of destruction his truck left, but not a god damned smudge where the fucker sat.

Convinced his mind had just hibernated for six months, Travis stumbled towards the nearby forestry where he had witnessed the lifeless body soar through the cold air like a sack of potatoes. He knew that the body had slid all the way across the road, yet the snow resting on the ground appeared undisturbed and continued to accumulate as if nothing had happened.

Travis had no clue what had happened. Did he fall asleep and dream the whole thing? Did he hallucinate it? One thing he did know is that his crazy bitch soon-to-be ex-wife could never find out about this. In the custody hearing that was sure to follow, she would tell the judge how Kyle's friend had almost lost his leg, and how four boys were damn near killed as part of Travis's "mental instability". That was a sure way to end up with only weekend visitation rights in the best of scenarios. Regardless of what had *actually* happened, he needed to come up with something to tell the kids. They were all napping when he had decided to wake them in a sliding death box, so no one saw a thing. He stomped back towards the truck with pure disgust towards himself and his head hung low. The boys, with the exception of Brian, had gathered on the passenger side looking for any indication of what Travis was searching for.

"You gonna tell us what happened?" Kyle demanded.

With the feeling now running out of his legs, Travis snapped out of his trance. "A dog was sitting in the road and I had to swerve out of the way," he told them flatly, trying to keep a firm complexion.

"A dog?" Mikey questioned. "Out here? We're in the middle of nowhere."

"It doesn't matter right now," Jimmy interrupted. "Brian is passed out and bleeding more. We need to get him to the hospital now!"

Travis had heard enough. "Everyone in the truck now!" He hated losing control of a situation and this one had all but vanished from his grip. "Brian is our priority. I'll explain everything later." They all piled back into the truck. Brian was situated back in his spot, lying across the back seat, unconscious. Travis trotted around the truck back to the driver side and caught his own reflection staring back at him in the window. *The years have taken their toll.* Bags under the eyes, a few gray hairs freckled into his sea of brown. It seemed like only last week he came to the cabin as a boy with his parents.

"Dad!" Kyle brought Travis out of his nostalgia. "We need to go!"

Travis opened his door and slid back behind the wheel to find the engine idling. "God dammit, I didn't even turn off the truck." He felt helpless, as if he were watching himself in a dream, but couldn't control his actions.

"It's fine, please start driving," Brian croaked from the back seat, startling everyone else in the truck. "I feel like shit."

Awkward silence blanketed the truck as Travis began to cruise back along the road. Jimmy gave Brian some potato chips to help with the hunger, which was probably making him feel worse.

"I'm sorry this all happened, boys," he said in a confessional tone. "Something is going on and I wanted to be sure that we're okay to go home. Brian, I'm going straight to the hospital, so hang in there."

Brian groaned in pain. For the next several minutes they remained in silence as they all listened to the steady hum of the engine, wondering what the hell had happened with Travis. His own mind also wandered while he drove.

I know what I saw. I think we're being followed right now and I know who it is. Travis leaned back and thought about his mother. She always had an answer.

2

"Seven more weeks," Tracy Stephens whispered under her breath. She pulled the coffee pot out she had just refilled and worked her way back to the restaurant floor. She strolled by Rodrigo and Antonio, the cooks who always yelled Spanish obscenities to each other while flipping eggs and bacon.

Tracy had become immune to the smells of eggs, pancakes, bacon, and pretty much any breakfast food that filled the air within the confines of the Denny's establishment. She had worked there since August when she had moved from San Diego to begin school at Denver State University (DSU). The deal she made with her parents consisted of them paying for her $10,000 per semester tuition, as long as she covered all other expenses, including books and rent. She had seven more weeks until the spring semester ended and then she could quit her God-awful job and return to Mommy and Daddy's house for the summer.

With the DSU campus located in the heart of downtown Denver, life didn't come cheap for Tracy. She had survived this far on free Denny's meals and a five-hundred dollar check every two weeks with some measly tips thrown in.

Her return in the fall to start the second year concerned her the most. People from all over the country flooded to Denver thanks to legalized marijuana and trendy technology companies expanding their offices into the Mile High City. This led to skyrocketing rental rates, especially in the downtown area. Tracy rented a 500 square foot studio apartment about half a mile from campus. Her landlord had already warned her that the rent would likely double by the time she returned in the fall.

Due to this, she started to familiarize herself with some of the suburbs right outside of Denver. The city of Grant seemed a likely candidate with a fifteen minute drive to the city and reasonable rental rates for the time being. Grant was a suburb that had benefited from the economic boom in Denver. Once a smaller suburb and home to average income families, the city had grown into an expensive and rapidly expanding community. New schools, hospitals, and even a strip mall had popped up in the past year due to the growth in population.

Her father, Chet, tried talking Tracy into attending a school that was not in the center of the bustling city. DSU had everything she could ask for, from the beautiful campus overlooking the city, and an energy and passion on campus unmatched by any of the other schools she had toured.

Chet outlined the pros and cons for each school within Colorado since he insisted she move out of state to "experience life". A Jesuit college just outside of downtown offered plenty, but the thought of being hounded by religious nuts for four years was too much. Boulder had the reputation as the party capital of colleges, but what was the point of school if you had a hangover every day?

Denver State had felt like home from the beginning and Tracy wanted it no other way. She had her grades right where she wanted, the friends she needed, and the rent money to have a place to sleep.

This particular Tuesday night, when the homesickness

started to kick in, she had some unforeseen excitement come her way. Since her classes ended in the early afternoons, she no longer found the second leg of her double shift to be as tiresome as it was when she had a full day of classes. Pushing eggs and filling coffee mugs in the middle of the night thanks to the graveyard shift didn't exactly challenge her. If she needed to work tired, hungover, or just plain unmotivated, it was quite easy for her to do so. As was the case every late night shift, drunken college kids would tumble in around two in the morning in dire need of grease to soak up the alcohol they had consumed all night at the bars. Entertainment never lacked in these special moments; she even looked forward to it.

Girls would spill their life stories and guys would hit on her non-stop. She tried her best to look unappealing by leaving her makeup off, but all that seemed to get her were creepy compliments about her beautiful green eyes. Just a "part of the job" her manager informed her.

Tracy topped off a coffee for a middle-aged man who appeared to be on a "lunch" break for his own graveyard shift. As she turned away from his table, she froze at the sight of blaring headlights that illuminated the restaurant through the front windows. The light remained for about ten seconds before disappearing back into the still darkness of 1 a.m.

Tracy felt the blood rush into her gut. *It's him!*

Around this same time during her shift the previous night, Tracy sat in a booth with a customer and learned all about his life. His name was Cole, a young twenty-something fresh out of college currently working a late night shift in a customer service call center for Netflix.

Tracy reciprocated by opening up to Cole about the struggles of trying to live up to her father's expectations, the hate she was developing for her job, and the overall love she had grown for the city of Denver during her stay.

Then, the conversation took a deep turn. Cole wore a long, tan parka with a matching fedora cocked low enough to shade most of his face. The weather wasn't nearly cold enough to warrant a jacket. "So what gives?" Tracy lightly asked. Cole confessed that he had a rare skin condition called Argyria that caused his skin to turn a slightly gray tint at random times. Embarrassed by this, Cole explained it was why he always tried to cover up his skin and used the hat to cover his face. His disease wasn't severe, so the graying condition came and went like strangers passing by. This particular night appeared to have no problems as he showed off his regular, pale skin.

Tracy developed instant sympathy upon discovering this disease. Her little brother had burned his face in an accident and lived with a scar shaped like Florida smacked across his cheek. She understood the struggle of people afraid to live in their own skin.

They continued to swap stories and Tracy was overcome with emotion from learning of Cole's past. He spoke of being beaten, burned, and nearly murdered in middle school due to his condition. The school staff nor his parents seemed to give two shits and left him to fend for himself.

As the countless and horrific stories piled up, Tracy felt as if she were listening to a Holocaust survivor speak of the unthinkable terrors they experienced while trying to survive.

Tracy wanted nothing more than to be there for Cole, as by the sound of it, he still lacked someone in his life he could count on. No friends, not even acquaintances. She also felt intrigued by him. For all he had gone through, he still had a gentle demeanor to go along with the mysterious vibe, and a persona that steamed out of his jacket and fedora.

With her emotions strung high, Tracy stood up from the booth before she ended up chatting with Cole for her entire shift. Cole stared up at her, startled by her sudden movement.

"Did I say something wrong?" he shakily asked.

"Of course not, but I'm at work," she explained as she looked around the empty restaurant. Cole glared around and met her eyes again with a small grin on his face.

"I see how it is," Cole said in a much more confident tone. "I see you're a busy woman. Pretty, too. I get it. But, I like talking to you. Just throwing it out there." Her face blushed as she gave a coy smile in response, brushing back her dirty blonde hair behind her ear.

"Tell you what," Cole continued. "I want you to think things over. I know you will anyway, as you're a college smarty pants after all. I'm going to leave now, but I'll be back at the same time tomorrow night.

"I'll come to the same booth. If you're interested in seeing me outside of these walls, bring me a milkshake. Chocolate please. If you want to keep this friendly and confined to these walls, bring me a coffee."

A romantic! Tracy looked away like a little girl embarrassed to talk about the cute boys in school. Cole rose from the booth and slapped down a twenty on the table for a tab that was only seven dollars and some change.

"See you tomorrow!" she finally said. Cole gave a tight-lipped smile, headed down the maze of tables, and out of the front door.

Tracy couldn't wipe the smile off her face as she picked up Cole's table. She would indeed do some thinking on her way home.

* * * * *

The early morning passed and Tracy finally went home for some sleep before her late morning classes. She tossed and turned all night, waking to find the sheets a tangled mess. Her mind seemed to gravitate towards Cole, even when she tried her hardest to think about anything else. Since sleep avoided her, she decided to commence her internal debate on the chocolate shake versus the Cup of Joe.

Well, he's cute in his own weird sort of way. He seems pretty together for having such a rough childhood. She turned on her TV for some noise and distraction. Late night reruns of *The Office* played and kept her entertained. *I just want a Jim and Pam kind of relationship. But it's hard since I never have any free time. I don't know if I should even be getting into a relationship before leaving for home for three months. If it's meant to be, it's meant to be and it will happen. If he's still around when I come back in the fall, then that's a sign.*

Only the conscience could talk itself out of what it had already decided against. She fell asleep while she thought about pouring coffee into Cole's mug, but hoped the summer would not send him completely out of her life. They could still talk, but a long distance relationship was simply out of the question, even if only for a few months.

She woke up groggy and out of sorts, needing at least two additional hours of sleep, but class awaited. The day at school dragged and she felt like a zombie crawling across a deserted highway looking for anyone to eat. She couldn't recall a single lesson during her classes, but she also hadn't thought back to Cole either. The grind of the semester always took its toll, but one night of bad sleep could throw the whole thing into overdrive.

She thought God threw her a bone, cancelling her last class of the day, which left her with two and a half hours to take a nap in her car before work. Thanks to running late in the morning, she had no choice but to park in the school's multilevel parking garage which was always cool, quiet, and dark.

She reached her midnight blue Mustang that her Daddy bought for her as a high school graduation gift and collapsed into the reclined front seat, having no issues sleeping. Her dormant mind didn't even wake her to the sounds of screeching cars and loud mouthed students that passed.

When she awoke from her phone alarm, drool dripped down her cheek in a stream. *Time for this* fucking *job.* She still hadn't let Cole back into her mind, partly because she knew he wouldn't arrive at the restaurant until the rest of the world was a good two hours into their night's snooze.

The dinner rush brought the usual crying babies and cranky parents that looked even more tired than she felt. She put on her best fake smile as the "power hour" from six to seven provided the biggest opportunity for tips. She ran when her hands were free and made sure to check on every table in her section every ten minutes. *A friendly face doesn't mean anything if they don't get to see it,* her manager recited one of his usual cheesy quotes.

Dinner fizzled into a smaller dessert crowd of people wanting to eat some pie before returning home for the evening. Once the pie people left, the restaurant may as well have been a morgue. Between ten and midnight she'd be lucky to have one table. After that a small boost of graveyard shift workers came in on their lunch breaks and an entertaining crowd of drunk college students.

She tended to a couple of businessmen who rushed through their meals when the bright headlights flooded the building, blinding Tracy for a moment as she picked up the dishes from the businessmen's table. When the lights flickered off she glanced at her watch and realized it was a few minutes past 1 a.m.

Cole, she just knew it. Nerves rattled through her body as her mind raced.

Hopefully he would understand why she wanted to stay friends for the time being while she tried to figure out her life. She understood that may not be likely as many guys had strong opinions against the "friend zone".

Tracy skirted into the kitchen to get out of sight from the main floor. She heard the front door creak open and chime its bell, giving way to a subtle shuffle of feet walking by her hiding spot. She peeked around the corner and saw the same booth from the previous night occupied by a man in a long, tan parka with a matching fedora. His back was facing her, but who else dressed like that at this time of year?

The coffee machine chimed to indicate its latest brew had finished. Tracy strolled over and poured the fresh coffee into a mug to take out to Cole, awaiting his disappointment. She sighed as the coffee reached the brim, knowing she would need to let Cole down easily so as not to ruin anyone's night.

Tracy grabbed the mug and walked back onto the main floor, striding straight towards the same booth with her shoulders held high and a confident posture, oblivious to the businessmen who waved goodbye as they exited the restaurant.

She stayed silent as she approached, noticing his hands tucked under the table and his head staring down at the tabletop.

"Hi, Cole." Tracy faked an excited tone as she slid the mug into Cole's line of sight.

Silence.

She couldn't tell if he was looking at the coffee or not, since his fedora rested extra low tonight. He remained so still that Tracy had to fix her stare on him to ensure he was actually breathing.

"Cole, I can explain." Tracy couldn't take the silence anymore.

"What the fuck is this?" a flat voice questioned from below the fedora. Still no movement. Tracy took a step back from the table, not expecting such a harsh response.

"I thought we had something going," the emotionless voice continued. "We had a good time and you had to go and talk yourself out of a great thing."

"Cole, please let-"

"I suggest you stop talking. Save your nonsense about 'not being ready in life right now' for someone who gives a shit!"

"What?" Cole's accurate statement caught Tracy off guard. "How did you-"

"I know *everything*," Cole continued. "You can't keep anything from me. You're not sure about your life? Well, I'll help to answer some of those questions tonight." The voice remained steady and unwavering. He still showed no signs of movement, keeping the brim of his hat low enough to shade his entire face.

"I thought this would be cordial, but I guess I was wrong," Tracy mustered out in a nervous tone. The anger radiated off of him like an atomic bomb.

"I know... I know how you *wanted* it to be, but you fucked it up," Cole continued without movement. Tracy stared down into the darkness cast over his face, wondering what was happening behind that shadow.

The restaurant was eerily deserted, and she didn't expect any of the drunk college kids for another hour. Tracy looked around at the empty chairs and booths, patiently awaiting her next move. She knew her cooks were in the back of the kitchen watching soccer on their phones like any other night along with her fellow waitress for the night (in case things got busy), Yolanda, who never worked too hard during these late shifts.

"I think I'll be leaving now." Cole rose from the booth in a swift motion. "Perhaps you'd like to join me?" He snatched Tracy's arm just below her elbow, pulling her in closer towards his face. The hand felt cold, dead, against her skin as he towered over her. His breath reeked of chewing tobacco and that nearly made Tracy vomit all over herself, but she kept her composure.

Cole removed his fedora, revealing his dark gray skin and beady, black eyes staring at her. His lips parted in a grin, revealing a set of charcoal black teeth.

A shriek froze in Tracy's throat that she could not force out. She felt as if she had no control over her mind or body after Cole had grasped her. It felt like her body was running on autopilot.

Cole released his grip on her arm, throwing her a couple steps backwards. "I said I want to talk...outside," Cole demanded, flashing his black teeth in an evil smile. This time she saw the sharp points of the teeth, similar to those she imagined a werewolf to have.

Tracy took advantage of her freedom and bolted for the kitchen where she knew she would have a numbers advantage over Cole. She screeched to a halt once she crossed the entryway of the kitchen and shrieked with all of her might.

Behind the industrial stoves and ovens, lying on the back wall next to the freezer was Rodrigo with his throat slit wide open, as if smiling at Tracy. His once white apron had turned a deep shade of red, almost black, from the amount of blood he had lost. Next to Rodrigo, splayed out face down on the ground was Antonio. A puddle of brains and blood formed around his head.

Tracy wondered where Yolanda was. She could be dead or hiding, but had no way of knowing for sure. A sense of loneliness clenched its ugly teeth around Tracy's already paranoid mind. She turned back out of the kitchen and sprinted for the front door, banging a couple of chairs out of the way en route to her freedom.

The moonlight glowed over the still night as Tracy burst through the front doors of the Denny's. She stumbled onto the pavement of the parking lot and gathered her footing, panting, out of breath. Her hands fumbled in her pocket, searching for her car keys while she dragged her feet down the front sidewalk of the building. That feeling of puppy love towards Cole had vanished like a balloon in a hurricane and gave way to a much stronger sense of terror. The night felt eerily quiet until her keys made their ever faithful jingle and she clutched them with a fist, yanking them out of her jeans pocket.

With the sense of security her keys brought, Tracy broke into a sprint around the corner of the building, giving a quick glance to confirm Cole had not followed her out of the restaurant. Employees were required to park in the back parking lot behind the building where the overflow spaces often filled up on busy Sunday mornings after the church rush. Otherwise, it served as an unofficial "employees only" lot.

When Tracy turned the corner that led into this lot she froze to see Cole leaning against her Mustang, one foot on the front bumper and both hands on the hood behind him.

He must have come out the backdoor through the kitchen. She would have too, if not for the blood-covered floor and two dead bodies laying there like roadkill on the side of the freeway.

"Sweet ride you have here," Cole's voice came out cold, slightly raspy. "All I wanted was to talk outside, but you *insisted* on causing a scene."

"Get the fuck away from me!" Tracy shouted with hopes of attracting the attention of some poor soul that might happen to pass by at this time of night.

"Oh, I'll be out of your way in no time," Cole responded calmly, with a devilish smirk. Even in the dark, she could see those black, rotting teeth that looked like fangs.

He stood up straight and extended a hand towards Tracy. "Now, come here so we can have a discussion...please!"

Tracy felt her legs move forward below her. The feeling of no control engulfed her once again. After five steps she tumbled and fell within a couple feet of Cole. Her keys that she held in her hands flew out of sight as she caught herself, scraping her palms in the process.

"Sorry about your cook friends. I didn't want any distractions, just some quality alone time for me and you," Cole said, and then howled up towards the moon.

Oh, my God, please don't let me get raped. Please, please, please.

"You think we'll do *what*? Rape? Physically impossible for us to do, so don't flatter yourself."

We? Us? It's just him, she thought, while getting some relief from his words.

Tracy rolled over onto her back hoping not to get any more scrapes than she already had from falling. Cole promptly swung his foot back and rammed it into Tracy's face. Blood gushed out of her nose and onto the pavement below her. Her head rang and her vision came in and out of focus.

She lay still, which didn't *feel* very still due to her head spinning. She could hear Cole laughing, sounding as if he was coming from every angle around her. It felt like there were ten of him circled around her, laughing at her like a ring of bullies gathered around their innocent prey.

Dear God, please send someone to save me, she began to pray.

"Pleeease," she whined. "Leave me, please!"

"You're going nowhere, bitch!" Cole barked. He reached inside his parka and retrieved a cleaver, which looked like the one from the Denny's kitchen. He held it up into the night, catching a reflection of his own smile on the blade.

"I thought about letting you go tonight. I really did. But then I thought on it some more, much like you did." Cole knelt down beside Tracy's head so he could speak into her face.

"I guess I had a change of heart, so you aren't leaving me tonight until I say so." Cole grinned in her face, revealing those hellish teeth. Tears rolled down Tracy's blood-soaked cheeks. *I'm going to die tonight.*

"I really do like your car. Would you mind if I borrow it later?" Cole casually asked, like a friend would.

"Cole, please. Why are you doing this to me?" Tracy pleaded in a low, desperate tone.

"Let's just say I'm doing you a favor," Cole responded and stood above her head. "You'll be leaving before the fun really begins and you'll be glad. It's going to be ugly."

Cole stared down into Tracy's eyes and for a brief moment she believed that he felt compassion towards her. He gave a kind smile, then quickly shot his hands above his head with a tight grip on the cleaver.

"Nooooooo!" Tracy shrieked. Cole slammed the cleaver down

and sunk it deep into Tracy's left thigh. A faint *clink* sound could be heard as the blade made contact with her femur. She had that feeling again. The screaming and agony caught in her throat like a fly in a spider's web while her hands grasped her bleeding thigh and could only muster a grunt from a pain she had never experienced.

"Fuck you!" she cried out as if her throat had been released from a chokehold. Cole smiled as he swung the cleaver down again, this time into her forearm, immobilizing her.

"Tonight you die!" Cole shouted into the calm night. He picked up the keys to the Mustang that Tracy had flung only moments ago. The keys glimmered in the moonlight conveniently next to the driver side door of the vehicle. The night blacked out his face as he looked down at her, creating a silhouette of his broad frame that led up to his fedora in a pit of darkness.

"My apologies for the mess tonight, Tracy, but *you* asked for it," he growled at her as he opened the car door.

Instantly, the engine roared to life and the high beams flashed across the lot. Tracy felt the cool grip that death had wrapped around her, and the headlights did nothing more than complete what she imagined the "bright lights" to look like at the end of it all.

Cole floored the accelerator, making the Mustang scream and squeal into the silent night. He howled like a lunatic as he repeatedly punched the steering wheel.

The revving ended abruptly, leaving Tracy to hear only the sound of crickets chirping and her own heavy breathing. She lay flat on her back staring up at the full moon, praying one more time for someone to rescue her. Out of the corner of her eye she could see the front end of her car inching towards her head.

The feeling in her legs fled like a burglar from a crime scene. She wiggled her fingers and felt pain shoot through her whole arm. So much blood had formed a pool by her legs that it spread towards her face. The car stopped a foot away from her head, continuing its gentle, idle hum. She closed her eyes, took a deep breath, and let more tears stream down her face, making a new puddle of their own as they dripped off her quivering lips.

In the far distance she thought she heard police sirens, but she had no way of knowing if they were for her. The high beams continued to blind her, but she could still sense her car's proximity and the warmth radiating off the engine.

Just kill me already. All hope had fled from her, as she realized her prayers would not be answered. The sirens grew louder along with Tracy's heart beat as if trying to burst out of her chest.

"Nice knowing you, Tracy!" Cole shouted out of the driver's window. "Thank your daddy for the sweet ride, I'll take good care of her!"

Tracy channeled all of her energy to roll over to no avail. She returned to the paralyzed state from earlier, lying on the ground helpless, and she watched as smoke rose from the fiercely spinning wheels of her own car. The smell of burnt rubber on the concrete grew so intense, she started to gag.

Cole released his foot from the Mustang's brake and the car jerked forward. Over the roar of the engine, a loud cracking sound similar to the sound a tree makes just before falling over echoed throughout the lot. He smiled at this thought.

Tracy's head exploded underneath the tire like a balloon, causing her brains to stick all over the front bumper.

Cole sped out of the parking lot, cackling as he admired

Tracy's flattened, headless body in the rear-view mirror. As he pulled onto the main road, the sight in that same mirror gave way to blazing red and white lights.

"Oh piggy!" Cole screamed. "Why yes, I'd love some company!" He accelerated the car to triple digits and headed towards the freeway entrance.

3

Susan Wells sat on her back porch and sighed. She scratched her head in frustration, a good reason why the gray had finally won the battle against the jet black in the war for what was once a head of luscious hair. Her restless fingers drummed against the laptop she had just closed, now resting on her lap.

She couldn't ask for a more beautiful day. Birds sang above the freshly cut lawn. Kids giggled and screamed during recess at the school a couple of blocks away, and not a single cloud visited the sky, leaving Susan's wrinkled skin to soak in every ray of sunshine; a perfect spring day in Larkwood, Colorado.

Susan slid on her reading glasses, which were clipped to the collar of her shirt, and picked up her Samsung smartphone from the table. Her grandson, Kyle, thought it was the coolest thing that his grandmother used computers and cellphones, as many of his peers couldn't say the same of their bingo card stamping grandmothers.

Susan reread an email she had just received from her boss. An unfortunate situation had arisen, but fortunately for everyone involved, she had dealt with a similar event back in the eighties. They needed her expertise, and since this particular scenario only came by every thirty years or so, she figured this would be her last trip around the Ferris Wheel.

As far as anyone knew, Susan worked as an executive at the

local Coca-Cola offices. In reality, the government recruited her out of college in 1972, when she was still Susan Miller, to join a special task force led and founded by President Nixon, referred to as "Operation Z" at the time. Over the years, as the force grew and became more honorable and prestigious, members started referring to the team as The Crew.

The Crew recruited special types of people. Creative, free thinkers with strong survival instincts and a killer mindset was only the beginning. Once these traits were identified, individuals would then go through vigorous aptitude testing. Complex word problems would be provided, and one would need to respond with the answer but show how they arrived at that solution in multiple ways. Susan finished her packet of one hundred of these word problems in a two-week span, which was one of the fastest times recorded in department history.

Members of The Crew weren't required to be in any sort of physical shape, but rather to have quick reflexes. Once graduated from the written exam, candidates would be placed into an obstacle course type of maze in Washington D.C. for a test of physical abilities, reaction time, and further cognitive ability in working through the maze.

Most candidates would need an average of eight hours to complete all tasks and find their way out. Susan completed everything in three hours and twenty-six minutes, which to this day is still the best recorded time.

While some candidates would waste blocks of thirty minutes at a time walking in a large circle, Susan understood the purpose of the maze circled around completing the tasks as they all led to the eventual exit, and not only finding the way out. She only took the route in the maze that led to the next obstacle, which became more and more difficult.

Each obstacle proved to be nothing more than real life word problems. Tasks such as statistical analysis that required the use of advanced Algebra were the base of every obstacle. The challenges along the course only required critical thinking and a strong capability of completing math within the head, something Susan had long success with. The word problems carried more weight than what she remembered from elementary. The first question within the maze asked her to calculate each American's worth based on factors of Gross Domestic Product, incomes, costs of living, and a list of other information provided. Each obstacle was set up on a round table to allow multiple people to solve it at the same time, but she found herself alone each time as she moved by them with ease. With Susan's quick mind, navigating through the fifteen obstacles gave her no issues. President Nixon even made an appearance to witness Susan complete the maze once they realized her pace would shatter records.

Upon setting the record, Susan was immediately escorted to the White House for a meeting in the Oval Office with President Nixon. Her palms welled up with sweat as she couldn't believe where she was going. Just two weeks earlier she had been the first of her family to graduate from college. That followed with a job hunt where she didn't find much success.

Her temporary misfortune flipped a one-eighty when an all black business card appeared on her car dashboard after a trip to the grocery store. It read, "Call for work" and had a number below in silver lettering. Needing an income, she called the following day for more details. A monotone voice answered and described the work as a government job, not providing much information. It all sounded sketchy as he refused to give her thorough details about the job, but he did say if she passed the round of personality and critical thinking tests that would arrive in the mail, they would fly her out to D.C. for further review in person.

She took the tests that arrived in a plain, unmarked manila envelope. Even the test avoided hinting at the job duties, but it did make it clear that the job would be top secret as it questioned heavily around loyalty. She mailed the test back the next day, not expecting much, growing convinced the card left on her car was all part of some scheme to extract personal information.

But they didn't, she thought. *There was no request for my phone number, social, nothing. Only my name. I didn't even give them my address and they still mailed the test here.*

Susan had learned of the *laissez-faire* approach of the U.S. government, but never once underestimated its capabilities and power.

Her flashback came and went as the unmarked government car she rode in (driven by a man named Stevens), turned into a driveway and pulled up to an armed gate where two men in suits that screamed Secret Service waved them through.

She craned her neck as the car crept at an almost pedestrian pace. Trees towered all around her. She couldn't see where they were, but she knew. For being such an iconic building in the middle of the city, they sure managed to hide it well.

The car made its way around a never-ending loop and she finally saw the house that she had only ever seen in pictures: the White House. The elegance took her breath away. She no longer felt nervous, but rather a feeling of disbelief took over. Was this really happening? Susan Miller at the White House by the President's escort service? She prayed every night and tried to live out her life everyday as a woman of God, so this type of experience humbled her in a way she never imagined.

Stevens helped her out of the backseat when the car pulled up to the door of the White House. She had never realized an entry door sat below the iconic six pillars of its rounded entrance. She also had always thought this area to be the building's front, but Stevens informed her it was technically the back door of the house. He led her through the door where two more Secret Servicemen nodded in unison as they passed. Portraits of past Presidents watched them as they walked down the hall towards the Oval Office. The polished hardwood gave way to carpet beneath their feet, giving Susan the sense of walking through a typical office space as they entered the main corridor of the Oval Office.

Stevens approached the closed door and knocked three times with a crisp fist. "Mr. President, Ms. Miller is here." He awaited a mumble from the other side of the door, pushed the door open, and took a step back to welcome her into the Oval Office. When she entered, she noticed the navy blue carpet that covered the entire room. The walls were a pristine white, likely scrubbed every day by the lucky person with the task assigned to them, and the rest of the decorations were all a golden mustard color. The couches that rested parallel from each other, creating a walkway to the President's desk, matched the drapes that hung behind the desk, as well as the Presidential seal imprinted in front.

President Nixon stood at his desk. The light glowing through the windows behind him let Susan only see his silhouette until she approached closer. "Susan, please have a seat," he welcomed her with an extended hand as he walked around his desk. He seemed antsy, but not quite nervous, despite keeping a demanding, yet relaxed tone. *Just part of the job, I'm sure.*

"Welcome. I'm glad you were able to make it out and do

so well at our assessments. Can I get you anything before we start?"

The President asking me if I want anything? God, help me!

"No thank you, Mr. President." She did her best to not sound like a giddy teenage girl which she wasn't too far removed from to begin with. Her eyes crawled all over the office, still in shock that they were seeing the inside of the actual Oval Office. She noticed the portrait of George Washington that hung over the fireplace, the flags for all military branches to the side of the desk, and she even caught a glimpse of a golden doorknob that stuck out of the wall, which was an obvious secret door. "One thing I would like, Mr. President, is to know what this is all about."

"Naturally," he responded in a flat voice with a sharp grin as he returned to his seat. "That's why you're here. Now please sit."

She sat down in the mustard chair that faced his desk. *Oh my, Elvis sat in this same chair a couple years ago. I remember seeing it in the papers!*

The desk made him feel quite a distance away with its sheer width. The rich mahogany glowed with its perfect polish. She couldn't help but notice the bulging, manila envelope that laid on the edge closest to her. He pulled out the first page and handed it to her.

"This is an offer letter to join our secret operation," he said.

Her eyes jumped to a handwritten annual salary of $350,000. No typos there. A 23-year-old woman making more money than the President? What's the catch?

President Nixon explained the job in detail as she trembled with the offer letter in hand. He stressed that joining this special task force put her life in immediate danger, but that

38

was the reason behind the intensive testing. "If you think the testing is hard, wait until you see the actual training for our program," he smirked, which made her uncomfortable. "Our goal is to make sure no one's life is truly in danger because of how tried and true the training methods are."

He explained the risks of death associated with the job, and informed her that she could be killed on the job as well as executed for speaking with anyone regarding her work, with a few exceptions. He spoke to their main tasks as hunting down foreign beings that posed threats to not just the United States, but the entire world. Operation Z was top secret, and not even Vice President Gerald Ford would learn of the task force until he took over the Presidency.

The final clause he addressed was the term of the position. Lifetime. Quitting was not an option and retirement did not exist in this position, at least not in the traditional sense. This employment expired when her death arrived, whether on the job or not. She would have to consent to a tracker chip being implanted into her back to remove any chance of running away once the pressures of the job mounted. The government wanted to always know each member's physical location. Property of the good ol' U.S. of A.

"Mr. President, I need some time to think this over," Susan said, still trembling with so many thoughts trampling through her mind.

"I completely understand," Nixon responded with a sly grin. "This is more than a job; it's a lifetime commitment."

"I can't believe this is a real opportunity for me." Susan flipped through the pages, shaking her head in disbelief.

"You're special, Susan," the President stroked her ego. "You have talents and gifts unlike anything I've seen. I have a bigger vision for you if you join, and yes, you'd be compensated even more."

"Bigger in what sense?" Susan grew even more intrigued as the conversation progressed. The thought that she could earn even more money was borderline unbearable for her.

"Well, this is a brand new sect of our military, clearly top secret," Nixon informed her. "We'll be needing a leader for the entire branch. While it's not a position I can just give you, as you'd need to prove yourself first, it does appear you have what it takes judging by your test scores."

Already getting promoted before accepting the first job? Not a bad gig.

"Oh, and your salary would be tripled in this potential role." That statement hung in the air for so long Susan was tempted to reach up and grab it.

"Well, Mr. President, you've made it very hard for me to deny this opportunity," Susan said as he rose from his seat, prompting her to follow. "I'd still like a couple days to sleep on this and be sure."

"Of course, take your time." The President had no issue understanding the nature of this request. "We'll send the contract to your house so you can review it at your leisure. Keep in mind the nature of this position, and don't discuss with anyone...we'll know if you do."

"Thank you, Sir," Susan extended her hand to meet the President's and then she shook it firmly, trying to not seem terrified by his last statement.

"No, thank you. My contact information will be in your packet, so please don't hesitate if you have any questions. I like to keep this team close to my chest," the President said as he guided Susan out of the Oval Office.

She was escorted through a back way out of the White House by two men she believed to be Secret Service. The place crawled with them. The two men led her back to the black town car where Stevens awaited to drive her back to the airport for her return flight to Denver.

As part of the Presidential treatment and final touch of the sales pitch, Susan was driven directly to a private plane appointed by Nixon around the back of the airport. No time to waste standing in security. Stevens loaded her two bags in her overhead bin and vanished without a word spoken.

Now this is a life I could get used to, she thought as she reclined in her seat. *First class treatment, a huge paycheck, and the direct phone number for the President of the United States. Why wouldn't I take this?* Despite the excitement and anxiety she felt, airplanes always made her drowsy and craving sleep, even the fancy ones apparently.

Forty years later, her government-issued cell phone buzzed on the kitchen table, bringing her back from her original White House memories. She missed her late husband, Robert, wishing to talk to him about the old days when they worked together for The Crew. President Nixon was long gone, but The Crew lived on, strong as ever. The new man in charge, Colonel Griffins, was calling, and her stomach dropped at the sight of his name on the screen.

4

Travis doze at the wheel. Even with all the excitement that had just occurred, all the boys had managed to fall asleep again, leaving him in a moving box of silence. The digital clock on the truck's panel read 7:45 p.m. Kind of early for middle school boys to be exhausted, but that is the price they pay for staying up until six in the morning and only sleeping a handful of hours the entire weekend.

Travis had his own fatigue issues to deal with, and shook his head to try and release them. After going to bed at a responsible time of 11 p.m. the previous night, he found himself unable to fall asleep. The voice in his head caused more of a disturbance than the random outbursts of laughter by the boys hanging out in the living room.

His upcoming divorce took control of his mind the second he laid down and it refused to let him fall asleep. Coming up to the mountains always helped him clear his mind. After nineteen years of marriage, being alone at this stage of life terrified Travis, especially since he didn't know the first thing about dating or even meeting people in the technology reliant world of today. *Do I really have to go online to meet people?*

His mother's words played over and over in his head from their last conversation only a week ago. "God gives you nothing you can't handle," he repeated to himself as he tossed and turned in bed.

His mother always came through with a spiritual quote to apply to life's current happenings. She insisted that religion and faith in the man upstairs kept her level-minded and normal throughout a chaotic life. "If you can't let go and let God, that's when you'll snap."

Regardless of the reasoning, Travis calculated a total night's sleep of three hours, leading to the exhaustion that he had difficulties fighting. He had the quiet, steady hum of the engine, and the back-and-forth motion of the windshield wipers to keep him hypnotized.

Travis slapped himself across each cheek to get some sort of jolt, and decided a trip down memory lane would help take his mind off of how tired he felt. Thinking back to the good old days always brought a smile to his face, and he could sure use that right now.

Since driving was the task at hand, he thought back to when he was a kid riding along with his father. He enjoyed the view from the backseat of his dad's old Chevy Impala. There were no seatbelts or rules to worry about back in the seventies. Travis attributed his toughness to growing up in this era, and loved to say that kids in today's world are "too soft". He came from a time where receiving a beating from his father was socially acceptable and no one dared to question it.

"The world sure has turned pussy," he whispered to himself with a proud smile.

One of his favorite memories of his father consisted of smoking cigars while driving. Travis loved getting a random whiff of smoke in the backseat. Watching the smoke dance out of the rolled down window always mesmerized him as a child. He could still smell that sweetness from the Romeo y Julieta cigars to this day.

Travis's mouth watered at the thought and he couldn't resist any longer. He reached over his sleeping son and opened the glove compartment. After some rummaging, he retrieved a small black box that was his homemade humidor, fully equipped with a moist paper towel inside. Keeping his eyes on the road, he reached into the box with one hand and brought a cigar to his nose.

That's the shit, he thought as a tear rolled down his cheek. He didn't smoke cigars often, but when he missed his dad more than usual he always lit up a tasty stogie. He stuffed the cigar between his lips, and being the purist his father taught him to be, pulled a pack of matches from his black box.

He held up the pack and saw the small writing that read "Fred's Diner". The diner was his and his father's favorite restaurant to visit. More tears came and with them more memories. Like Dean Martin said, "Sweet, sweet memories are made of this."

It became the tradition for Travis and his father to go to Fred's diner to watch every Monday Night Football game. This tradition carried on for over twenty years until his father became ill. Even still, they would watch the games together from his hospital room.

His dad passed away on a cold, drizzly Tuesday morning in December. Just hours after they had watched his beloved Denver Broncos on Monday night fight back for a thrilling come-from-behind victory led by John Elway. It just happened to be a month later that the Broncos went on to win the Super Bowl. To this day Travis still felt the wave of emotion which hit him like a sack of bricks on that Super Bowl Sunday. He sat in a booth at Fred's Diner by himself (as he insisted) and bawled his eyes out as various Broncos players passed around and kissed the Lombardi trophy.

The feeling of draining within his chest that always accompanied heart ache returned as his eyes welled up with tears, temporarily blurring his vision. He wanted nothing more than to hug his father and get his advice regarding his crumbling marriage as he always had the perfect thing to say when it came to any scenario in life.

Talking to the gravestone of Robert Wells and getting no response always drove Travis to the brink of depression. The concept of physically sitting above his father who rested peacefully underground made him sick to the stomach. It reached the point where his visits to the cemetery became less frequent due to the overwhelming sense of disappointment he felt every time he had to leave. Only the dead could spend the entire day at the cemetery, and he was sure to remind himself of that fact to force himself to walk away.

He lost all focus on the road as he reminisced, but fortunately traffic wasn't exactly rush hour at the moment. He wiped the tears with his sleeve and regained his composure, taking one final puff of his cigar and flicking the remaining stub out into the blizzard.

He began feeling normal again. For a brief moment he forgot all about his pending divorce, Brian's bleeding leg, and even the fact that they had fled his cabin due to a madman in the woods. He looked over at Kyle sleeping in the passenger seat with his head against the window and knew everything would work out for the best.

He returned his focus to the road and the faintest flicker of a light appeared in the mirror. After a double take Travis determined the lights belonged to a moving vehicle.

His heart sank at the thought of another car appearing on the road after they had been on the road for over an hour. Where could it have come from? They hadn't passed any intersections or towns, just more trees in the middle of nowhere being swallowed up by swirling snow. The distraction brought Travis back from his diner memories where he could still smell the combination of fried potatoes and some sort of cleaning chemical that always seemed present inside the walls of Fred's Diner. He could feel his father's presence warming him, just like when they sat cozily in the diner booth watching football.

The uncertainty started to spread, however, and Travis accelerated the truck to try and maintain the lengthy distance that currently stood between himself and the other vehicle. His knuckles turned white from the death grip he now had on the wheel, and he once again thought back to his mother, planning to call her as soon as he had cell phone reception.

5

"Susan, we have a code 10," Colonel Griffins said bluntly over the phone. "They're right in your own backyard. We need you."

The colonel was not one for small talk and liked to get right to the point, especially in a time of need.

Susan was technically retired from daily activities of The Crew, but being a lifetime commitment, she still needed to keep up with the current events of her task force. Retirement meant no longer checking in with colonels and generals, or her favorite, no more conference calls where nothing ever seemed to get accomplished. She did, however, need to maintain her knowledge of current happenings, and if the phone rang from Washington, she damn well better answer it to avoid an unpleasant visitor to her home.

The only reason The Crew would contact her during retirement would be to suit up for battle, something she was well aware of, and at the ripe age of sixty-three, she knew this would be her final battle.

The Crew had grown into one of the biggest secret sectors of the United States government, which studied, tracked, and followed extraterrestrial life.

A species of advanced human beings had been discovered in orbit around Mars in a spacecraft that looked similar to modern day satellites during the early sixties. President Kennedy started the efforts to create a task force similar to The Crew, but was assassinated shortly before an official launch. He kept the matter hidden, not even Vice President Johnson had any knowledge of it, meaning the idea had died with him.

It wasn't until President Nixon took the office when some documents were discovered deep within the confines of the White House. He found thousands of pages of research on this species referred to as the Exalls. The Exalls had technological advances unheard of by anyone on Earth, and certainly decades ahead of the times. The most peculiar fact about the species was that they did not inhabit any planet. They lived on the massive spacecraft that traveled throughout the galaxy.

The astronomers hired by President Kennedy could never locate exactly how far this spacecraft traveled beyond the depths of the Milky Way.

According to one astronomer, they determined the spacecraft returned to the proximity of Earth roughly every thirty to forty years. A note from President Kennedy addressed a concern for the security of American and global citizens a week before his death. The note was buried with the rest of the research and hidden until it was found years later, leaving the question of who else knew of the President's top secret plans and had gone out of their way to hide them.

President Nixon read over the notes and obsessed as he learned more facts about the foreign species. Further studies found that some members of the Exalls had invaded a small town in Pennsylvania in the late fifties. Reports were dug up from the town called Dalmatia. Newspaper clippings included in the file showed graphic images of a massacre at a gas station in the middle of town. The article explained that masked men in body length jackets opened fire with automatic weapons, killing six people and blowing the gas station to pieces. The two men were never captured nor seen around town again.

It couldn't be completely determined that the Exalls were responsible, but the intelligence concluded it to be likely. This provided a glimpse into the massive amounts of research conducted, and convinced President Nixon that a next attack would come some time in the eighties, which sparked the launch of The Crew to continue research as well as provide protection should any attack occur.

All of this led to the present day with Susan receiving a call from Colonel Griffins in which he commanded she prepare for her second battle against the Exalls.

"Yes, Colonel Griffins, I'm ready and have everything I need," Susan responded sternly. "I have my equipment, but I'll give it a second look to be sure."

"Perfect. I know you'll do well like you always have. Re-inforcements will arrive tomorrow," Colonel Griffins replied. "Godspeed, Sue."

Susan hung up her phone, placed it on the table, and cried. As she calmed down, the silence filled her head, so she prayed a quick Hail Mary. She thought back to 1983 when she had led the first ever defense squad to attack the Exalls on American soil. She was young, strong, and fast. Robert was still alive and fought beside her. Now, none of that was true.

Years later, after much physical regression and the advanced technology produced by The Crew, they still couldn't determine *when* the Exalls would begin their descent to Earth. Their stealthy spacecraft vanished from the sight of the radars in a gesture of the Exalls flexing their technological muscles. The Exall Tracking Devices (ETDs) could only sense them once they had set foot on Earth. This left them stuck in a reactive situation rather than being able to take a proactive approach. Fortunately, at this point, they could pinpoint the Exalls' exact locations. The radar in the ETDs used temperature to find the locations as it dropped an average of five degrees within the area when any Exall would be present. Similar to infrared, the radars used by The Crew also measured radiant energy. With data to support that Exalls possessed a much lower amount of energy output than a typical human being, The Crew could plant the exact coordinates of any of their extraterrestrial friends.

Susan got the chills every time she turned on her tracking device and saw roughly fifty Exalls spread across the world. The Crew had deemed most of them as not a threat, and a handful they simply could not reach due to international regulations.

They walk among us, she always reminded herself. *They could be the old lady in the back of the church. The cashier at the grocery store. I'll keep God close, but keep my gun closer.*

What troubled her worried mind the most about these fifty "unreachables" was that two Exalls were rarely ever together, seeming as if they did not even know of each other's existence. This made Susan think there was a whole other level to the Exalls' game plan that everyone had overlooked. With other proof that their species always traveled together the majority of the time, it left her to ponder what exactly this scattered group was up to.

Currently, Susan had no time to worry about such things. Exalls were in the mountains and in Denver, leaving her as the leader of the impending attack. Reinforcements would arrive in a few days from all around the country and they would need to be strategically placed in different locations around the city based on her orders.

As the highest ranking (and most senior Crew member in

Colorado), all of the preparation fell on her shoulders. This responsibility had long been the only duty she truly dreaded. Yes, she was a strategist by nature and loved game planning for their defense and attacks, but found the consultative work to be more of a burden than battling out in the field.

Susan had trouble sleeping over the past two weeks. It was no secret the Exalls had returned and were in Colorado. She had seen the emails and even checked her tracking device. The plan was to be long gone well before they arrived again after all these years, but life had continued into her golden years. With an impending battle right around the corner, she began to have nightmares.

Her dreams often consisted of being ambushed by the Exalls and kidnapped, always in a different setting. A school, a football stadium, and a deserted mall stuck in her head the clearest. Every time she would storm into the Exalls' location only to find no one present, she was then grabbed from behind, and woke up with sweat-soaked pajamas in the middle of the night.

Susan had long been a devout Catholic and attended Sunday mass regularly. When the nightmares had started, she went to mass on a daily basis. Every feeling in her gut told her it would not end well this time around. The Exalls became smarter and stronger every time they returned and would eventually reach a point where even the United States government would not be able to keep up.

All worry aside, she took comfort in the fact that this would be her final time fighting off these bastards. True retirement was right around the corner knowing there wouldn't be another Exall attack in her life time. All that awaited her were beaches, frozen drinks, and not a damn worry in the world except for what time Days of Our Lives would come on the tube.

She supposed she would take a long vacation after it was all said and done. They hadn't been on a big family vacation in a couple of years when she had taken the family to Italy for two weeks. A celebration to cap off a long career would be the perfect occasion for two more weeks in Europe or on a beach on some island she would never pronounce correctly. She had money stashed away, tons of it, and planned on paying for everyone's expenses once again. So why not go wild and spend Euros like there is no tomorrow? She would book the trip as soon as Colonel Griffins called her to declare the end of the battle.

Susan returned to her laptop and opened the tracking application she had helped create over thirty years ago. She glared at the small red dots on the screen that represented the Exalls and zoomed in on the map to show Colorado and found two Exalls together right outside of Golden while another flew solo within the Golden city limits.

According to Crew guidelines put in place during the previous war, she could not simply storm into Golden and start shooting them. Backup needed to be in place before any attack was to be carried out. They created these policies for good reason. In the previous invasion, four separate solo attacks were authorized, and all four of those Crew members did not make it home for dinner that night. The gory and unpleasant scene led to President Reagan's implementation of the new policy the following day.

Rules were rules no matter how bad she wanted to break them. Death as a consequence gave plenty of reason to hold back on her urges. She slammed her laptop shut and rose from the seat with her joints cracking and popping to remind her of her age.

Susan carried her laptop and shuffled out of the kitchen down the small hardwood hallway towards her office, which looked as if a soul had never worked in it, even though she spent a majority of her time working there.

A massive maplewood desk rested against the back wall, which reminded her of the Oval Office. She could see her reflection when she looked down at the desk thanks to the constant cleaning and polishing. The only items on top of her desk were two computer monitors, the keyboard, and the mouse. She always made a point to clean up after working or surfing the internet.

A cozy, black leather office chair on wheels sat atop a black and gray freckled rug above the hardwood.

"I was really hoping not to do this again," she said into the empty room. Susan rolled the office chair aside towards a filing cabinet that watched her from the side wall, and bent down to fold the rug back, revealing a small door outlined in the hardwood. The outline blended seamlessly with the rest of the flooring with only a small handle embedded into the surface. Susan tugged on the handle to raise the door open.

A musty smell filled the room as this door had remained closed for nearly twenty years. Inside the small hole in the floor laid thick books that contained information and strategy on fighting Exalls, most of which she had written. Next to the stack of books rested a cluster of guns from pistols to shotguns, and of course her favorite, the assault rifle buried at the bottom. She never advocated for guns but grew an appreciation after they had saved her life numerous times in the first war.

Folded neatly beside the guns was an armor suit equipped to handle anything from bullets to knives, yet which still provided great flexibility to maneuver. A utility belt attached to the suit contained a night vision scope, a couple of small knives, and rounds of extra ammunition.

Susan pulled out a book from the stack and flipped open the hard cover. An index-sized card presented itself with the image of Saint Michael thrusting a spear into a demon. The back of the card contained part of a verse of her favorite Psalm: *"Deliver me and rescue me from many waters, from the hands of aliens."*

The card faded and the white became a light yellow to show its age. It was the same card she had tucked in her vest during her previous war against the Exalls. She put the card back into the inside cover and closed it, wanting to make sure it was still there after having it custom-made when she initially joined The Crew, and knowing she would need it later. She even had it blessed by her hometown priest, Father Tom.

Susan survived some intensive training and near-death experiences and never hesitated to give thanks to the Patron Saint of Protection she kept stashed in her front pocket. She was done with the inventory check and returned the book into the hole in the floor, replacing the door and rug back over, leaving the office as innocent as it had looked a few minutes ago.

Thoughts consumed her mind as she stood in silence in the office. Only her son and her late husband knew the truth of her job, but she had lied to Travis, insisting she would never have to fight again. He needed to know the news; it was only a matter of finding the right time to deliver it.

She had six days until she would be out leading a squad of six Crew members. It was currently a Sunday and her grandson, Kyle, had his basketball team's end of season ceremony and party on Friday, the day before her war began. Travis would be there and she could pull him aside to tell him the truth. He would have plenty of questions so she would need to deliver the news earlier in the day rather than dropping the bomb on him before bed time.

She had played out the conversation multiple times in her head over the past couple of weeks and now she needed to execute it. The importance of him keeping it a secret for the sake of everyone's lives would be stressed once again.

Susan remembered that Travis and the boys went to the cabin for the weekend, and hurried back to the kitchen where she left her phone. The dots connected in her mind that the Exalls were also in the mountains, in that general area. They would certainly be out for revenge on Susan, and she knew that. They easily had the capability to track down her family and torture them if they wanted. Her knowledge of the Exalls comforted her slightly as she knew they would not harm them without her presence.

These were cold, ruthless beings. If they planned to hurt her children or grandchild they would ensure that Susan would watch the whole thing.

Nonetheless, she would call Travis to check on things. Her call attempt sent her directly to voicemail without a ring.

Could be a dead zone. Could be out of battery. No reason to panic.

Susan had been a mother for nearly forty years and she still worried about the smallest issues. She tried a second call attempt only to receive the same response.

Her eyes stared down at her phone on the table and she started to panic.

6

Officer Zachary Lopez patrolled the streets of downtown Denver, waiting for something to happen. Weeknights rarely presented opportunities for him, but he never let that get him down. This particular Wednesday night was no different. He started his graveyard shift at ten o'clock, and his watch informed him the early morning was now approaching one o'clock on Thursday morning.

Being a Wednesday night, Zachary patrolled the neighborhood known as the Ballpark District where nightclubs and bars filled the area centered around Coors Field, home of baseball's Colorado Rockies. Wednesdays were popular for "ladies nights" at various bars around the area and he always came prepared to keep an eye out for any stumbling women that late night prowlers might try to take advantage of. Not that it was illegal to hit on drunk girls, but he knew his mere presence could prevent a situation from escalating out of control.

At the age of twenty-nine, Zachary wasn't far removed from the downtown nightlife. Just three years previously he found himself on the scene on a regular basis. Fresh out of college and enrolled in the police academy, he worked a day job of cleaning cars for a local dealership. He lived by himself, kept bills to a minimum, and most importantly, he had no college debt. His money at that time pretty much went to paying the rent and buying drinks for pretty ladies he met at bars.

He spent his free time at the gym when he wasn't getting phone numbers or working. Ever since high school he had wanted to become a police officer. During his freshman year he enrolled into an Intro to Government class. While politics didn't exactly appeal to him, they did lead him to branching out his own research into the country's legal system. He would spend hours after school exploring Wikipedia. One click always led to another and a new page full of more possibilities, and because of that, he taught himself more about Colorado law then any other teenager could possibly know.

Zachary was raised by a single mother of three. Seeing her determination and working three jobs on a daily basis provided all the motivation he needed to work hard in life. Having three jobs caused some absurd shifts at times. His mother would come home from one job, cook dinner for the kids at around five o'clock, and leave by six for her next shift, which wouldn't end until three in the morning. She once mentioned that a police officer that patrolled the area of her work would always escort her to her car in the early morning hours. The neighborhood had some gang problems, so the officer was always glad to be of assistance.

Hearing this story sparked his initial interest in law enforcement. With so many negative stories in the news regarding police brutality and racial profiling, he grew adamant that plenty more good was being done than bad, and people simply didn't hear about it. The opportunity of being a protector for the community drove his work ethic every day.

One Saturday night after a long day of written exams at the academy, Zach decided to have a night out downtown for some drinks. His mother raised him to be independent, so when friends were unavailable, he had no problem going out by himself. He dressed in the classiest suits he could afford and always got a haircut Saturday morning to have a fresh fade before going out. He had no problem filling in his suit thanks to a rigorous weight lifting routine, and his mother always told him he looked like a Mexican drug lord whenever he went out with his dark skin against the white suits.

Midnight approached as he sat at the bar of a nightclub called the Mile High Club, a popular hangout for college students that attended Denver State. The club was always jam packed on weekends and trying to zigzag through the herds of people flooding the dance floor proved to be an accomplishment in itself. If the bathroom was needed, he could expect another ten minute wait after fighting through the masses to reach the line for entry.

The club was massive; in fact, the biggest in the city in terms of physical size. It had three levels, each playing different music and with different drink specials. The decor provided a classy feel with grand chandeliers that hung from the ceiling and reflections off the disco balls that danced across the club. Golden lighting illuminated the ground and paved a walkway to easily access the different sections of the club, even though the crowds of people spilled onto the path. All paths led to the bar, of course, which was tucked comfortably along the back wall in a semicircle. Three bartenders manned the station as the lines for drinks remained constant all the way through the last call for alcohol. The Mile High Club attracted the best bartenders in town, as they could expect to earn at least four hundred dollars on Friday and Saturday nights each. To pull in that money meant working fast and never getting distracted. Zach would often sit at the bar for a few moments and chat up his main bartender, Charlie. Charlie had the fastest hands Zach had ever seen make drinks, and being a regular at the club, Charlie always had a Jack and Coke ready for Zach once he saw him enter the club.

On this particular night, upon taking his seat and checking in with Charlie, Zach noticed a woman across the bar. She sat by herself and kept running her index finger around the rim of an empty glass. She had the perfect shade of brown skin, and long flowing golden brown hair that hung over the left side of her face. Her slouch suggested disappointment from what Zach could tell.

"Hey Charlie, what was that girl drinking?" Zach asked and nodded towards her.

"She had a double vodka soda. She seems bothered by something," Charlie explained. Bartenders have that way of always knowing what's going on whether they speak to you or not.

"Send her another, on me," Zach said as he stood up from his seat.

"You got it, boss." Charlie flipped a glass in the air, scooped it into the freezer of ice cubes, and was already pouring in vodka and soda by the time he pushed his chair in. She would have a drink in her hand before Zach could even walk across to her - that's how fast Charlie was.

Zach walked with a stiff posture around the bar, squeezing between a couple groups of people and approached the beautiful woman as she took her first sip of her refilled drink. As he came within arms reach he noticed her perfectly fitted black dress that accentuated every curve of her body. Her mocha-colored legs led down to sparkling black high heels that complemented her dress. Her head was turned away from Zach, so he caught himself staring her up and down before realizing what a creep he must look like. She started to slightly bob her head to the new Usher song that boomed through the club's speakers. Zach's heart beat rapidly at the sight of this, feeling instant compatibility with a total stranger.

"Hi there," he shouted to be heard over the music. Zach had perfected his craft in getting women to at least converse with him after going through trial and error at least a couple hundred times throughout college. His first rule was to never make any physical contact until she initiated it. No hugs, high fives, or even fist bumps unless she reached out for one first. Maintaining space developed a safe zone that allowed trust to grow, and once that was in place the conversation seemed to flow in a more relaxed manner.

She turned around to find Zach standing a couple feet away from her. He noticed her eyes scanning him, forming that first impression. She gave him a soft smile and said, "Hello, what's your name?" in an even softer voice.

"My name is Zach," he said, putting an open hand to his chest. "And what's your name?"

"Cristal," she responded a little more loudly. She extended a hand to Zach to shake.

Never fails, he thought as he shook her hand, feeling skin so soft it reminded him of a small stuffed animal.

From that point they talked the night away, eventually going to the club's outdoor patio so they wouldn't need to yell over the music. They learned the basics about each other, such as favorite music, movies, and so on. Cristal was in her final semester at Denver State, close to finishing with a degree in Hospitality and Hotel Management. Zach's mother managed a small motel so they chatted about hotel life for quite a while.

As the conversation carried on and the alcohol kept flowing throughout the night, the two shared deeper feelings. Zach discussed his father leaving him and his siblings behind, and the fire that burned deeply in his heart towards him for ditching his family. Cristal countered with the extreme pressure put on her by her parents to succeed in school. They had immigrated from Mexico just before Cristal was born with the hopes of their daughter having the opportunity at the "American Dream". Her parents struggled once they moved to the States, jumping from job to job while trying to earn their American citizenship. It took fifteen years before they were sworn in as citizens of the United States of America, making job security much easier and they were finally able to dig themselves out of financial hell after another five years. Because of these struggles, Cristal worked at a Burger King through high school, saving all of her money for college. She contributed every now and then to help out with groceries and bills, but they insisted on her saving for college since they could not help.

She finished high school with a 3.8 GPA and earned a decent-sized scholarship to attend Denver State. She coupled this with another scholarship designated for first generation Americans. The money she had saved during high school went towards books and entertainment for her college years. Long nights of studying, turning down friends, and becoming a social outcast resulted as part of her determination to graduate as soon as possible. Seeing her parents struggle pushed her every minute of the day to ensure a better future for herself and them.

Cristal became fascinated with a bed and breakfast home that she had the privilege of staying in while on a trip to the mountains with some fellow honor roll students in high school. Their host was an immigrant from Guatemala, named Izabella, who left an abusive husband and fled for America in the hopes of turning her life around. After a night of arguing turned sour, Izabella snuck into her husband's closet and took a secret stash of money he had hidden. She had stumbled across the money one day when gathering laundry from the closet and never told him that she knew about it. The night she left, she had more than 700,000 Guatemalan Quetzal in her bags, equivalent to 100,000 American dollars. In the eighties, that money stretched a long way and helped to purchase the house she currently ran as a bed and breakfast. Business took off for Izabella and she was able to buy another home about thirty minutes away, and operated that as a second business. Hearing her life story led Cristal to ask more and more questions, and she eventually decided that she also wanted to run a bed and breakfast of her own one day. Her parents could help with the cleaning and maintenance of the property and they could all share the income together. This was her main plan and pursuing a degree in Hospitality only gave her more tools as she looked into real estate for an available house.

Zach offered his mother as an available resource and this earned him a tight hug from his new friend.

"I like talking to you," he said clearly, giving every effort to not let the alcohol cause a mumble. "I want to take you on a real date tomorrow night."

Cristal smiled and looked down towards the ground. "Okay, let's do it. Pick me up at six. I'll text you my address."

"Well, it's bedtime now," Zach said as he his watch informed him it was quarter past two in the morning. "I'll see you tomorrow."

"I can't wait!" Cristal responded as she stood up and gave Zach one more hug for the road.

One date led to another. And another. Within a year they had moved in together in a brand new apartment building downtown. Zach entered the police force and Cristal was in the early stages of preparing her newly purchased house for a bed and breakfast grand opening. The two were married about a year after confirming they could handle living together.

Zach always replayed these events in his mind every time he drove by the Mile High Club. This night was no different. He usually drove by the club on purpose when time allowed, as it had a sentimental hold over him. The night was quiet, so he drove around downtown, pondering life. Weeknights rarely presented any excitement, but he carried on with high hopes.

Officer Lopez was fairly new to the police force, having been sworn in just over a year prior. He had a fire burning deep within to excel at his position of law enforcement and believed no idle time should be taken while on the job. Being proactive and searching for something to do had long been a part of his work ethic, and having a quiet night always brought that quality out of him.

On the rare free time he would enjoy, he visited with local business owners and residents in an effort to immerse himself into the community. He wanted to be a "go to" person that the community could rely on and he considered this constant socializing crucial to becoming just that. He often thought about running for mayor of Denver in the future, and realized that would require hard work with the police force and a growing popularity among future supporters.

His charming and outgoing personality came naturally. It was impossible for him to go out anywhere in public without striking up a conversation with a stranger. He began his mission on the very first day on the job, meeting every resident in the downtown neighborhood he was patrolling. He gave everyone his direct office phone number to contact if they ever needed anything. His wife considered this a blessing and a curse. She saw that he would have plenty of support should he ever decide to run for office, but at the same time, she often requested they go to dinner outside of Denver for the sake of having a private, uninterrupted conversation. Zach had become somewhat of a celebrity in the community, getting stopped anywhere the couple went. Zach planned on two dinner outings each week with his wife outside of the Denver city limits. It was his time to unwind from the energetic person he was while on the clock and have a quality conversation with Cristal.

This cold April night was sure to influence his career and future, and become a night to remember for the rest of his life. Static blared on his radio, bringing him out of his deep thought and soaring his excitement.

"Calling all units in the University area, we have a 187 at the Denny's restaurant across from campus. There are two dead in the kitchen and one survivor hiding in the pantry. Over," the static voice spoke quickly and clearly.

"Ten four, I'm on it, en route." Zach snatched his radio eagerly and responded.

"Copy, Officer Lopez, suspect is described as tall, wearing a tan parka coat with a fedora, no further description. Survivor not sure where he went, use caution. Coroner will be there shortly, please create a perimeter. Over and out."

Zach was already headed in the direction of the Denny's but still a couple of miles away. He flicked on his sirens and emergency lights to clear the path towards the restaurant. Only two cars appeared on the road ahead and they both pulled aside promptly upon hearing the sirens.

Sweat accumulated on Zach's palms as he sped down the road. Catching a murderer on a quiet night like this could propel his career in law enforcement and he didn't want to let the chance slip away.

He wanted nothing more than to call Cristal and share his excitement, as twisted as it may be, but he knew better than to wake her at one in the morning on a work night. He had made that mistake once before and quickly learned that you do not wake up the wife of a police officer in the middle of the night as she will only assume the worst.

The squad car approached the restaurant, the yellow glow of the Denny's sign now visible. Zach could see through the windows of the restaurant and realized no one was inside the dining area. He also noticed a car with its headlights on, sitting idle on the side of the building. The lone headlights seemed to be staring at Zach, waiting for him to arrive.

The headlights jeered to the right and fled out of the parking lot, swerving onto the road in front of him. The driver quickly regained control of the vehicle, which appeared to be a dark-colored Ford Mustang from Zach's knowledge of tail lights. With the manner in which the car fled the scene, Zach had no choice but to take the leap of faith and assume it was the murderer making a run for it.

"I'm in pursuit of the suspect, driving a black or blue Ford Mustang," Lopez shouted into his radio. It could have very well been a nervous witness getting the hell out of there, but the fact they were accelerating away from a police car with lights and sirens blaring suggested otherwise.

It was a gamble Zach wanted to take. The potential rewards far outweighed the risks if the person he was pursuing was not the murderer. If it wasn't, the killer was likely already miles away from the crime scene whether Zach had stopped at the restaurant or not. If it was, though, he would be in line to receive an outpouring of recognition from the police chief and the community. It wasn't the medals or awards that Zach craved, it was advancement in his career, and he knew that capturing a runaway killer was a surefire way to a prosperous career, especially being so new to the force.

He didn't want fame, just a luxurious lifestyle for his future family. These goals and dreams were always in the back of his mind and subconsciously pushed him to capture the suspect as he followed the speeding Mustang onto the freeway entrance, heading north onto Interstate 25.

The pursuit officially qualified as a high speed chase and Zach lost all control of his nerves. His heart pounded profusely, adrenaline flooded his body, and he could feel the intensity of his pulsing hands on the steering wheel.

"It's go time!" he screamed to himself. "Go big or go home!"

The radio broadcasted screaming voices that he could hear over his own sirens. Some other officers had arrived to the Denny's and the chaos could be heard as the radio cut in and out. Zach learned that a woman had been flattened in the parking lot by a car and there were also two slaughtered bodies inside the restaurant's kitchen.

Zach's throat tightened upon hearing the gory description of the crime scene. This wasn't some accidental manslaughter suspect he was chasing; it was a cold blooded multi-victim murderer.

"Backup requested for hot pursuit, we're northbound on 25 from Speer," Zach trembled into the radio.

"Copy, backup is on the way," his dispatch snapped back. The weight of the world lifted off of his shoulders. As much as he wanted his shot at glory, the wise decision to handle this type of person would require some assistance.

With backup on the way, he only needed to worry about keeping pace with the fleeing car. He gained speed as he needed a closer look at the vehicle's license plate, and pointed his car's spotlight to focus on the plate, paying no attention to the darkness of the night that seemed to zip right by his line of vision.

With some confidence returning, Zach grabbed his radio. "I have a read on the plate. It is a California plate. I-L--"

He froze mid-sentence, not wanting to believe his eyes. Beads of sweat formed on his brow and the blaring sirens seemed to fade into background noise as his mind raced once again.

"Officer Lopez?" the radio crackled at him as he held his end to his lips. He couldn't break his stare from the license plate.

"Where the hell is the backup?" Zach's voice cracked. "We're approaching Park Avenue, get them here now!"

"Backup is approaching from 20th street. Officer Lopez, the plate number please," the now bitchy voice demanded of him.

"California plate I-L-K-I-L-L-U." He let the letters hang in the air.

"Copy."

Clearly his dispatcher did not figure out what that spelled out as silence now poured out of the radio. His mind felt as if it was on autopilot and the car drove itself. He maintained the speed with the Mustang, but had no sense of directing where his own car was going.

That damned license plate kept Zach in a trance with its scribbled red text of *California* hovered above the thick, blue lettering that threatened him directly. "I'll kill you," he whispered to himself, needing to hear it out loud. He felt light headed and thought he might be having an out of body experience.

He released his grip on the steering wheel and removed his foot from the accelerator. The car continued on uninterrupted. He stared in amazement at the steering wheel as it kept its subtle glide back and forth as if a ghost controlled it. The car then sped up as the Mustang started to gain some distance.

In a panic, Zach slammed on his brakes, and the car responded by speeding up even more. He snatched his radio with both hands and screamed in a piercing voice, "I have no control of my car. I repeat, no control!"

More silence.

"Hello!" he pleaded into the radio. "Hello anyone!"

As he stared into the radio console on his dashboard waiting for a response, his flashing lights and screaming sirens both shut off abruptly. He flicked at the corresponding switches to no avail. It was as if someone had pulled the plug on the car altogether, somehow cutting off the power to everything except the engine.

The patrol car hummed along as they proceeded down the freeway. The headlights did remain on and kept their focus on the back of the Mustang, despite Zach having no control. He repeatedly peered into his rear view mirror as he longed to see the flashing lights of his backup. His heart sank the longer they did not appear and all he kept seeing was darkness fading in and out as they zoomed by the streetlights standing tall above the highway's median.

"Where the fuck are you guys?" he screamed. He punched the car's horn and that appeared to be disabled as well.

Zach leaned over and rummaged through the glove compartment, pulling out his cell phone. He slid his thumb across the screen to unlock the phone, revealing a background picture of his new bride on their recent honeymoon. He had taken that picture upon their arrival at an all-inclusive resort in the Bahamas. Shortly before blessing their room for the first of many times that week, Zach captured a candid photo of Cristal looking over their balcony into the sun setting over the horizon of the ocean.

The photo was perfection in his eyes, not only capturing the moment, but also the natural beauty and grace of his wife. A soft smile, long hair caught in the ocean breeze, and her mesmerizing blue eyes provided everything Zach would ever need in a photo of her.

Breaking out of his nostalgia from the islands, he quickly dialed "Crissy" from his contacts menu. The phone rang repeatedly in his ear, driving him hysterical.

"C'mon answer! I'm dying!" He began sobbing as his patrol car accelerated above 110 according to the speedometer.

"You've reached Cristal. Sorry I can't talk now, but please leave a message at the beep," the voicemail recording told Zach. The familiar beep sounded in his ear and he sat in silence for five seconds.

"Crissy," he couldn't hide the crying tone stuck in his voice, and at this point he didn't care. He spoke in a slow, defeated tone. "I love you. Don't ever forget that. I don't think I'm making it through the night. Love again and don't be afraid. I love you forever."

The thought of his imminent death oddly calmed his nerves as he left the voicemail. Acceptance is the first step and he had made his peace with that fact.

Zach hung up the phone, kissed the photo on his homescreen,

and held the phone to his pounding heart. He tapped on the brake in a last effort to stop the car and immediately broke into tears as the car sped up. He whispered a Hail Mary and closed his eyes, laying his head back on the driver's seat head rest.

As he was about to dial 9-1-1 on his phone to see if dispatch would answer, he was distracted by a bright red glow that illuminated the inside of the patrol car and seemingly the entire night with it. The Mustang dropped its speed drastically, slammed on its brakes, and screeched across four lanes of freeway onto the left shoulder.

Zach's car followed the exact path of the Mustang as if commanded. Both cars jerked to a sudden stop in unison, causing smoke from the burnt rubber to fill the night air. He didn't even notice the smell as he rubbed the back of his neck due to some minor whiplash.

He sat frozen inside the patrol car. Shock and relief tangled within his emotions from what seemed to be a sure death to sitting safely on the side of the highway. Zach let out a deep exhale as the lights from the Mustang in front of him flicked off. They had stopped under an overpass, which left the only visible light in the area coming from his own headlights. He could hear his heart pounding in his ears as he sat in silence, and he could feel his pulse throbbing in his temples.

Zach gazed at the still Mustang in disbelief. In a robotic motion he raised his hand to the ignition and killed the patrol car's engine. The Mustang had apparently done the same already, leaving the two sitting in complete silence.

In the five minutes of pursuit they had managed to travel roughly eight miles north of downtown due to their drastic high speeds, finding themselves where the northern border of Grant connected with the start of Broomfield.

He was familiar with the city of Grant since he had his aunt and cousins who lived there as long as he could remember. He hadn't explored as far north as his current location, so he looked side to side through his car windows in search of anything recognizable, but he only saw darkness.

This particular stretch of highway had no surrounding civilization. The closest sign of life was only a couple of miles behind where the newest housing development sat on the side of highway. All he could manage to see in the foreground was a large, white sign with black lettering that read, "Stevenson Homes Coming Soon!"

The sense of being stranded in the middle of nowhere set an uneasy feeling within Zach's gut. He had already forgotten about the fact he was driven to this location under someone else's will. The failure of his radio and the disappearance of his backup felt like a distant memory already as his mind raced on what to do next.

"Okay, what are you up to?" Zach said as he flicked on the spotlight above his driver side mirror. He directed the light through the back window of the Mustang's black tint and managed to make out one solid figure in the driver's seat who appeared to be wearing some sort of hat.

He regained some confidence knowing this was a one-on-one scenario since no backup would be arriving. Had he been outnumbered, he would have to consider sitting there and waiting forever until his radio worked or turn around and leave. He could sense the danger radiating from the Mustang and subconsciously touched his gun in his utility belt.

He attempted his dispatcher one more time and threw his radio into the dashboard after the unsuccessful attempt, then pushed the power switch to the radio, turning it off for good.

"Alright, time to be the hero," Zach whispered to himself.

He swung open the door as hard as the hinges allowed, which rocked the rest of the car. The hard pavement of the highway greeted his leather boots as he stepped out of the patrol car.

The night air turned cold, not uncommon for the early spring, but it felt colder than normal for this particular night. No other cars drove by the vicinity, leaving the chirping of crickets as the only notable sound.

Zach had his pistol pointed towards the Mustang, but he didn't even remember removing it from its holster. He began to feel as if he were lost in a dreamlike state of mind.

"Come out of the car with your hands on your head!" Zach yelled as he tightened his grip on the pistol. The crickets fell silent and he could only hear the sound of his own breathing. His fingertips pulsed frantically on the cold steel of the gun.

The door of the Mustang swung open, revealing a pair of pale hands elevated in the air. Zach jerked his pointed pistol to the hands.

"I'm sorry, officer," said a deep voice from within the Mustang.

"Step out of the vehicle!" Zach barked back.

"Okay, relax. I'm going," the deep voice responded. A pair of brown leather dress shoes appeared and gave way to a large figure rising out of the Mustang. A pale face could be seen under a crooked tan fedora that matched the long parka the man wore.

Zach always felt good about his height, standing at six feet exactly. The large man in front of him, however, prompted him to look upward into his beady dark eyes that stared back at him.

"Hands on the car now!" Zach demanded. "You are under arrest on the suspicion of murder and for fleeing the scene of a crime."

The large man did as he was told and received his Miranda rights while Zach slapped on handcuffs around his wrists. Being out sized, he had flung himself towards the suspect, seized his arm, and yanked it behind his back while simultaneously securing the handcuff. He repeated the process for the suspect's second arm.

Smooth, he thought as he gained more confidence in his current actions.

The fedora had fallen off of the man's head when Zach had slammed him against the car, revealing black slicked back hair with a tint of grease glowing in the moonlight.

"Officer, I think you're making a mistake," the man told Zach with a slight giggle.

"We saw the scene you left back there. You're lucky to be alive right now!" Zach shouted as he yanked the man away from the Mustang and shoved him towards the patrol car.

The man grunted in discomfort as his feet slid across the pavement from car to car. Zach patted the man down, searching for anything the suspect may have in possession.

"Do you have any identification?" Zack questioned him.

"Nope," the man responded with a tight grin that revealed blackened teeth.

"What's your name?" Zach stared up into the suspect's eyes. The man paused for a while after this question.

"No name," he said, maintaining his grin.

"Okay," Zach said, tight-lipped. "We can figure this out at the station if you're not going to cooperate."

Zach flung open the backdoor of the patrol car and guided the large man into the backseat, pushing his head down with force. He did not resist, which typically happened, but Zach didn't notice since his adrenaline levels had given him a burst of extra strength.

"I'm ready for the ride, Officer Lopez," the man said calmly. "Buckled up and ready to go!"

Zach slammed the door on his face, but the pale man maintained his grin and stared straight ahead.

"What the hell is going on?" he whispered to himself as he trotted back to the Mustang. He needed to fetch the keys so no one could come by and leave with a free Mustang on the side of the highway. The keys rested on the driver's seat with a sparkling pink keychain holding the set together. Encrypted on the keychain in purple lettering was "TRACY".

Clearly not your car, big guy, but nice try, Zach thought as he picked up the keys. He closed the door and pressed the lock button on the dangling black remote control. The doors clicked in unison and the headlights flashed to confirm the car had been locked.

He returned to his patrol car to find the suspect laid across the backseat with his knees bent to fit comfortably between the doors. His parka appeared to be stretched to its boundaries due to his awkward position with his hands behind his back and his body squished into a back seat that wasn't quite big enough for him.

"Unbelievable!" Zach cried as he opened his door. He allowed his body to fall down into the driver's seat and strapped on his seat belt. As he looked over his shoulder to demand the man to sit up, snoring sounds came from the backseat.

"I'm not gonna fight with you any more at this point," Zach said with frustration. "Go ahead and sleep because when you wake up you'll be in jail, and not my problem."

Zach fired up his patrol car and the engine roared to life in the quiet night. He turned his radio power back on, hoping to give it one more chance.

"Dispatch, are you there?" he asked in monotone, not expecting a response. More silence filled the airwaves. "Well then, I guess I'll be surprising them down at the station."

He shifted the car into drive and pulled forward around the abandoned Mustang towards an emergency turn around in the median. The downtown lights glowed in the skyline as he crossed the median and Zach realized how far they had driven.

From this distance it would take roughly twenty minutes to return downtown, driving at a normal speed. With a sleeping giant in the back who *seemed* to not want to cause any problems, Zach decided to leave his sirens and emergency lights off. He had enough excitement for the night and driving normally would suffice at this time.

* * * * *

Only five minutes passed from the time Zach left the abandoned Mustang with a passed out murderer in his patrol car. A discomforted grunt came from the backseat, followed by the squeaking sound of the hard, plastic seating as the man shifted his body.

A quick glance into his rear-view mirror revealed the man sitting upright, hunched low, as he was physically too big for the backseat. The steel mesh netting between the front and back kept the two separated, but Zach could feel the stare from behind, burning into the back of his head.

"Why hello, officer," the man said sharply from the back, sending chills down Zach's spine.

"I'm taking you downtown for processing. You'll stop talking if you knew what was good for you," Zach said sternly to cover up his fear. The man cracked another smile while he held his stare through the criss-cross of netting.

"Oh, Zachary, you're a great cop," the man laughed.

He has no way of knowing my name, Zach thought as he glanced around the dashboard for anything that might have his name on it.

The man fell silent and this made Zach uneasy. He checked the rear-view mirror to make sure he was still sitting in his scrunched up position.

"It's too bad you can't reach anyone on your little radio," the man said. Zach caught a glimmer of light in his mirror but couldn't tell what it was. A sharp sound of the netting being ripped alerted Zach that the glimmer had come from a knife.

He shrieked as he slammed on the brakes. Like earlier, the car did not obey and kept pacing at the posted speed limit of fifty-five.

"I told you, you made a mistake," the man yelled with pleasure in his tone. "I killed that prude pancake flipping bitch and now you'll join her!"

A cold, pale hand reached through the netting and grasped Zach's forearm. The man's fingers felt like dry ice on his skin and caused his arm to go numb within seconds. He tried to scream, but the man's other hand swung around from the other side of his seat and clasped over his mouth to suffocate the scream before it could escape. The chains from the busted handcuffs dangled from each wrist, brushing against Zach's hands as he tried to loosen the man's grip from his mouth.

It didn't occur to Zach that the man had pulled apart his handcuffs in a showing of super strength. He felt all the energy drain from his body, and his mind lost focus. His awareness stayed intact, but his body was weak and his mind had the fuzzy feeling he remembered from his college days pulling all-nighters to either study or party.

The man relaxed his grip and slid both of his hands backwards to rest on Zach's shoulders in a strangely caring way. Zach had never released his grip on the steering wheel and now watched his hands control the vehicle fully aware that his mind was not telling his hands what to do.

He felt his head start to become heavy and began slow blinking. He had grown so tired he didn't even remember the presence of the man with hands on his shoulders who seemed to be lulling him to sleep.

"Good night," the man whispered so quietly he couldn't be heard over the hum of the engine.

The man sat back and released his grip from Zach's shoulders. Zach fell asleep and slouched back in the driver's seat, arms limp by his side. The steering wheel was unattended but the car remained in the correct lane.

The man clicked his seat belt after strapping it across his chest and sat cramped, only this time with more patience. He closed his eyes and covered his head with both arms crossed diagonally.

There was a brief pause in time while the man sat like this. The patrol car, which still maintained its speed, suddenly veered to the left, slamming into the median. Screeching sounds of metal exploded off the median barrier causing sparks to fly from the concrete wall. The car flipped over the median and completed two full rotations while air bound before landing, slamming down on its roof. The emergency lights exploded into hundreds of pieces of flying shrapnel, as did the windows, upon impact of the car's tumble across the lanes.

Zach had remained fastened in his seat belt when he fell asleep and now hung upside down in the overturned car. He remained unconscious as blood trickled off of his forehead and formed a small pool on the ceiling of his car.

The man in the back caught a piece of glass in his jugular. He plucked it out like a hair, examined the shard of glass, and flicked it away unfazed. He released the latch of the seat belt and brushed some shards of glass out of his hair. Being too large for the backseat, he didn't suspend in mid-air like his friend in the front. Rather, his head rested against the ceiling of the car, which gave support to the rest of his body. He wriggled his legs and rotated his torso until he found the right position to slide out of the open back window, which was scattered across the highway at the moment.

He emerged from the car head first, crawling onto the pavement. Once free, he pushed himself into a standing position and looked around the deserted highway in both directions.

Still no car in sight, and he liked it that way. After all, he did arrange to have the overpasses on the northern and southern ends of the highway collapsed, and clearly, his partners came through like he needed. Traffic would have been minimal at this time regularly, but no one would come across this "accident" until he *wanted* them to find it.

He skipped giddily to the front of the car and knelt down to look through the absent windshield to see Zach.

"Thanks for a memorable night, friend," he said casually. "They'll be coming for you soon. Your fellow piggies that is, so I really must be going now."

He stood up from his crouched position and broke into a sprint towards a small hill off the side of the highway, disappearing into the shadows of the night.

The lights on his dashboard and radio all flicked on back to life, as if someone had plugged them back into an outlet. Screaming voices cut in and out, blaring from the radio and waking Zach. He thought he heard his name called out, but couldn't be sure while he fought off the urge to faint.

Zach mustered enough strength to reach for his radio and placed it to his lips. "Send help...on 25...flipped over."

He saw the river of blood pouring from his head, forming a pool on the ceiling of his car, and that pushed him to lose consciousness for a second time. The ringing of sirens faded away as he thought about Cristal, praying he would see her again.

7

"God dammit!" Travis shouted and broke up the silence and light snoring within the truck.

"What's the matter?" Kyle asked as he yawned, still half asleep.

"The gas light came on and we're nowhere near a gas station," Travis snapped back. He slowed the truck, pulling off the road to the right hand side. In the commotion of their quick departure, Travis had forgotten to refill the gas tank.

"Huh?" Jimmy asked, dazed and confused.

"Out of gas," Kyle explained, sounding a little more together.

Mikey awoke from all the fuss, but remained still and slow blinked with an empty stare out of the window.

Brian mumbled something, but remained asleep. A soft clicking sound complemented the flashing emergency lights Travis had activated as he came to a complete stop.

"Don't worry, boys. I have some gas in the container that we use for the four wheelers," Travis said. "Just need a minute to dig it out of the back."

The previous summer Travis had bought two Yamaha ATVs for him and the boys to ride throughout the mountains on their camping trips. Fortunately, the heavy snowfall squashed any possibility of that as the ATVs were buried under three feet of snow. If that hadn't been the case, they would have found themselves in a stickier situation on their journey home.

Travis slid out of the truck, falling into shin-high snow. He slammed the door and glanced to the bed of the truck, piled high with all of their camping essentials.

The headlights that appeared earlier closed in on their distance, seeming to focus on Travis who was literally frozen in his tracks. He could tell the car was an early 2000s edition Ford Explorer that appeared in fairly decent shape considering the car would be almost fifteen-years-old.

The Explorer zoomed by at roughly fifty miles per hour by Travis's estimate. Between his eyes adjusting from the headlights and the speed of the car, he could only make out the figure of a person in the driver's seat.

"Driving alone in this snow at that speed?" he said aloud. "Good luck, asshole!" He looked on as the Explorer's tail lights disappeared into a winding road down the hill.

Travis trudged to the back of the truck to rummage through sleeping bags, coolers, and duffel bags full of clothes until he felt the cold, hard plastic of the gas container. He yanked it free of the organized mess, walked back to the gas tank on the driver side, opened it, and tilted the container upward to pour the gasoline.

The guzzling sound made Travis thirsty. He thought a drink right about now would go a long way in keeping his sanity. A strong 7 and 7 on the rocks would do the trick.

His quick daydream was cut off by the sound of an approaching car. He looked around until he noticed a set of headlights appear on the opposite side of the road. The car's high beams blinded Travis so he couldn't see anything. He shielded his eyes and stared down to the snow trying to clear the flashing white spots from his vision, only to look back up to see the vehicle speeding by, splashing shards of ice and slush all over him and his truck. He caught the tail end of the vehicle and recognized it as the same damned car that just drove by.

"Motherfucker!" he shouted as he brushed the slush off of his jacket and sweatpants. He had emptied the gas container and dropped it on the ground during his blinded confusion.

Travis snatched the container with frustration, tightened the tank lid to the standard two clicks, and slammed the miniature door shut, stomping back to the truck bed to reshuffle everything to fit as originally positioned.

Why did he drive back this way? You lost, jackass?

Travis thought about loading his rifle, but talked himself out of it, deciding that their arrival to the hospital needed to be the main priority. He hastened back to the driver's seat, nearly jumping in. Snowflakes snuck inside before he slammed the door, melting instantly from the truck's blasting heater.

"What's with that car?" Kyle asked nervously.

"Don't worry about it," Travis responded.

"Are they following us?" Jimmy asked, a slight tremble in his tone.

Travis turned his head to the right to see if Jimmy was being serious. "C'mon now, no one is following us. Let's get out of here." He turned the key in the ignition, felt the rumbling as the engine awoke from its nap, and was instantly relieved as the orange needle moved up to indicate a little above a quarter tank of gas. They only had ten more miles left to be out of the mountains, followed by fifteen more to reach Golden and find the local hospital.

I am outside of the truck for five minutes and this jackass is driving around lost, making these kids jump to conclusions. Who knows what the hell they were saying.

Travis rubbed his temples and craved that 7 and 7 even more. The boys could sense from his tone that the conversation regarding the mystery vehicle driving around would not be continued. They all sat in silence as Travis took the truck back onto the trail home. Jimmy played his portable gaming console, concentrating on a shootout in a car game while Mikey pulled out his laptop to begin a different game. Brian continued snoring, oblivious to all the events that had unfolded.

"How is his bleeding back there?" Travis interrupted the silence after a few minutes.

Mikey put down his laptop to examine Brian's leg. They had wrapped a fresh bandage around it while Travis filled the gas. The bleeding seemed to have ceased as the bandage remained its original clean white.

"Looks better...finally," Mikey said as he returned to his position on the floor of the truck and reopened his laptop.

"Thank God," said Travis. Brian's blood loss was nowhere near a critical level, but it seemed never-ending, pooling drop by drop like a leaky faucet.

The road expanded into two lanes in each direction, meaning they were less than five minutes from I-70. Even though the lanes weren't visible through the packed down snow, Travis knew the location thanks to the, "You are now leaving Sheephorn, Come Back and Visit" sign on the side of the road.

He switched over to the right lane as that would become the on-ramp for the freeway. His heart sank as he looked into the passenger side mirror and saw headlights behind them.

"Ok, boys, stay calm, because I think our friends are back," Travis said as he tried to remain calm himself. They caught his stare in the mirror and they all shuffled around in unison to look out of the back window.

Just like earlier, the headlights grew and approached at an alarming rate.

"Holy shit," Travis whispered under his breath. Within seconds the same Ford Explorer pulled up right next to the truck and slowed down to maintain speed with Travis.

The once white SUV had turned a tint of brown, clearly a consequence of driving in the given conditions. All three boys who were awake gawked at the vehicle next to them. Travis looked back and forth, needing to split his attention with the road.

It turns out there was a person in the passenger seat, and he stared them down. Upon first glance, he appeared to have a dark skin tone, but after a longer look it became clear that it had more of a grayish color, similar to that of an elephant. He watched them through a pair of sunglasses that complemented a solid black cap tucked low over his brow.

"These are clearly some pranksters trying to get a laugh," Travis said calmly.

The gray man raised a fist towards the boys and shot up his middle finger. The driver of the Explorer threw back his head in laughter to show his appreciation for the gesture.

The Explorer sped up and left them out of sight promptly following the obscenity, causing an outburst of laughter, which awoke Brian from his extensive nap.

"What's going on?" Brian mumbled, half asleep.

"These clowns in gray makeup drove by and flipped us off," Kyle explained, trying to contain his laughter.

"Gray?" Brian asked with a serious tone. "Guys, I'm starting to remember what happened to me back there." Brian once again seemed calm and in control of his emotions.

He grimaced as he sat up, sliding his legs so they would

remain elevated, and he kept his hand rested lightly on his bandage as he began explaining his story.

"A man with gray skin did this to me," Brian started. "I thought I saw a squirrel, which was strange out in this storm. I went into the tall trees to chase it and left after a couple of minutes when I couldn't find it. When I got out of the trees I heard a crunch in the snow like a footstep from behind me. When I turned around I got drilled in the face with a snowball. It spun me around, then I got hit again in the back of my head, which knocked me down.

"I yelled for you guys because I thought you were all messing with me. That's when this guy came over to me. He pulled out a knife and I started screaming. He cut my leg. He was covered, but when he raised the knife I noticed his arm looked gray because it matched the cloudy sky. The last thing I remember is seeing my blood in the snow.

"I have no idea how long I was out when I woke up again and started yelling for you guys when Kyle found me."

Tears streamed down Brian's face as he recounted this story. He was glad to be alive and only have a gash in his leg as it could have turned out much worse. Amputation, paralysis, or even death could have all been realistic possibilities, but some stitches and crutches would suffice. They all sat in silence as the truck took the on-ramp to the interstate, a few minutes from the hospital.

8

The Golden Medical Center (G.M.C.) looked quietly over the town of Golden in the cold, brisk night. The newly built hospital stood ten stories tall and illuminated the skyline among the Rocky Mountains.

With multiple wings throughout the building that focused on different medical fields, many doctors from around the world made their way to G.M.C. as a primary residence.

Dr. Hudson Klemens sat in his office on the fifth floor, the intensive care unit, with his door closed. His head rested in the palms of his hands while he rubbed ferociously at his temples. A migraine had nagged him all day and he popped two more pills to try and fight it.

Maybe if I could just go to sleep my brain wouldn't try to kill me.

Dr. Klemens hadn't slept in 24 hours due to a busy day filled with two surgeries and four new patients admitted due to a nasty car accident that had occurred on Sixth Avenue leading into Golden.

Part of the headache could be attributed to the fact that he had to deliver the unfortunate news of paralysis to a teenage boy earlier in the day. The boy attended a small high school in Denver and reached local fame as an up-and-coming basketball star. He rode shotgun in one of the cars involved in the car crash.

When T.J. Lightfoot learned he would never walk again, the air seemed to suck out of the room. His parents sobbed as the three hugged from his hospital bed. T.J. had a full ride scholarship lined up to play basketball for the University of Connecticut that he had signed at the mid-year point of his senior year in high school. He climbed his way to the twenty-ninth ranked recruit in the nation to gain attention from practically every college in the United States.

All dreams of playing professionally flew out of the window and he would need to find a new passion in life. Dr. Klemens felt sick to his stomach as he spoke to the Lightfoot family. The damage to his spine proved too severe for surgery to repair, and even with a reputation as a miracle worker, Dr. Klemens could not help. He took these rare cases to heart, which usually resulted in binge drinking to make the guilt go away.

He had started turning to the bottle while in medical school. The stress became too overbearing at times and he needed the edge relieved. High pressure situations always caused a headache and he found alcohol to be the only true medicine to help. If it weren't for his good friend, Jack Daniels, Dr. Klemens would have dropped out of medical school and been known as Hudson Klemens, the car salesman.

His natural knack for persuasion never left him as he could sell water to a fish. The money nor lifestyle of a doctor never called to him. He genuinely enjoyed helping people and wanted a life dedicated to doing just that. In college, medical school may as well have been the furthest thing from his mind, but he decided to take it on after weeks of reflection and multiple sessions with a University counselor. He began with nursing school and found his drive was for a much bigger calling in life.

He would have been happy and satisfied as a nurse, but he

wanted to make an impact in people's life decisions. He thrived as a go-to person for those seeking advice and that led him on a trip to Yale University to a pursue a Medical Doctorate.

Hudson quickly learned that a stressful four years awaited him, with free time coming at a premium. Between classes, studying, and a part-time job, he never had a moment to himself. His only friends were his classmates as they spent a majority of the day together. No time existed for girlfriends or sex, which left his only release to drown in a bottle of whisky.

On the rare free nights he would have every three weeks or so, he darted straight to his dorm room when classes ended and undressed within a minute. He then pulled out a bottle of whisky from under his bed and served a tall glass, neat.

Pizza would be ordered about halfway through the first glass. He would lie on his couch and listen to smooth jazz while CNN ran on the television muted, until a knock on the door prompted him to slip on his robe to pay the delivery man. Plenty more whisky awaited Hudson on the couch once he returned with a whole pie in hand. The nights passed by as both the pizza and whisky vanished, and he typically woke up the next morning sprawled out in an awkward position on his couch.

These special moments showed him the true beauty in not having a roommate, a standard he kept in life to this day. Dr. Klemens didn't mind pulling into an empty home in the middle of the night. If he had a wife, she would just sit around at home alone anyway. His marriage involved helping people every chance he could. He knew a woman existed out in the world who would take no issue with his usual fourteen hour workdays, but she hadn't come into his life yet. "Everybody loves somebody, someday" always popped into his head. His someday would come later in life, and he accepted that.

The clock on his desk ticked away past six in the evening. Dr. Klemens arrived at work at ten o'clock the previous night. He felt his brain burn as it fought off sleep from working non-stop for nearly an entire day.

The doctor stood up and stretched his arms while releasing a long yawn. An average man in terms of height, he scratched his head through his jet black hair with some white peppered in, which made him appear much older than the thirty-eight years he had lived.

Time to grab some food and go to bed.

Dr. Klemens walked towards his closed door, picked up his briefcase that laid on the ground, and opened the door. He flicked off the light switch and grabbed his jacket from the nearby hook on the wall. Darkness swarmed his office behind him as he stepped out into the hallway and closed the door behind him.

A couple of nurses waved goodbye as he proceeded down the hall towards the elevators.

"Good night, Nikki. Good night, Ashley. Thanks for your help today," Dr. Klemens said, no longer aware of his own conscience. He hadn't worked with Nikki and Ashley in nearly a week, but all the days and nights jumbled together in his mind. He couldn't recall the last time he had slept for six straight hours. As far as he knew, he had worked for a week straight. Rarely could he speak of the date, let alone the time, while working at the hospital.

The elevator motor hummed behind the large stainless steel doors as he patiently waited for its arrival. The familiar dinging sound accompanied the doors parting their ways, revealing an empty car as he shuffled his way inside and pressed the "P1" button on the panel. Fortunately, he had his own reserved parking space. In his current state of mind he may not have been able to find his car if he had to park in the common spots with everyone else.

The door opened again to the top level of the underground parking garage. A black Mercedes straight ahead flashed its lights as Dr. Klemens unlocked the doors from his remote. He maintained his modesty despite earning such a massive salary. He chose to live in a small studio downtown when he could have owned a mansion in the suburbs, and he always donated money to charities as he never had any free time to volunteer. However, he simply could not resist the appeal of an all-black convertible luxury vehicle, so he had bought a Mercedes and splurged a little more to add some shiny wheels.

Dr. Klemens shuffled towards his car and popped open the trunk to toss his briefcase inside and slammed the door shut. Another yawn escaped his mouth as he opened the car door and slid inside behind the wheel.

The temptation to sleep in his car called to him. He weighed his options and decided to go home. A glance at his watch told him he could sleep twelve hours in his own bed if his phone didn't ring; a concept that felt like winning the lottery.

He glanced in his rear-view mirror and noticed someone stepping out of the elevator behind him. His eyes peered as he tried to make out if he knew the person since the parking level was dedicated to hospital staff only. He couldn't determine anything, so jiggled his keys in the ignition to rev up the Mercedes engine.

The GPS built into the dashboard lit up with all the other lights. Dr. Klemens clicked on the "HOME" tab on the touch screen. He never messed around with traffic and always needed to know the quickest route. His two options to drive home were either the freeway or Sixth Avenue into the heart of downtown. If an accident slowed down either route, he took the alternate. If both were clear, he defaulted to Sixth.

This evening, an accident had caused delays on the freeway. As he placed his foot on the brake to shift into reverse, he noticed the person from the elevator standing directly behind his car, slightly illuminated by the red glow of his brake lights.

"Dr. Klemens, I think you dropped something," a man's voice called out, distorted through the windows.

The doctor twisted around for a better angle to see out the back window.

Did I drop my badge? He reached into his front pocket and felt his badge missing. *God dammit, I just want to go to bed.*

He turned the keys and ripped them from the ignition out of frustration. The door flung open as he stood up from the driver's seat.

"Hello, doctor," the man said. Dr. Klemens still couldn't make out who the person was and squinted for a better look. The ill-lit garage didn't help as the shadows cast darkness over the man's face.

"Hello, what is it you have?" Dr. Klemens asked forcefully.

"Looks like a badge with your face on it. Did you have a good day today, doctor?" The voice had an underlying coldness and sternness.

"I'm sorry, who are you?" he asked as he rubbed his eyes.

"Oh, I'm a long time custodian for the hospital," the man responded. "Don't you remember me?"

"I'm afraid I'm rarely outside of an operating room to even see a custodian, so I do apologize if I've ever ignored you," Dr. Klemens had sincerity in his voice. He once again shuffled his feet to approach the custodian, a clear sign of his overpowering fatigue. He stuck his hand out to shake. "I appreciate you tracking me down. What is your name?"

As he approached the man, the dim lighting revealed the custodial uniform he wore. A smile cracked on the man's face and revealed a dirty shade of teeth that blended in with the darkness. The doctor froze once his mind processed the custodian's skin.

His face had a dark shade, yet it looked pale at the same time. The man's hand grasped his in return and the doctor realized that the skin had a tint of gray. A stream of light revealed this truth right where the two men's hands conjoined.

Hyperpigmentation? Lichen disorder? The doctor ran through numerous skin disorders in his mind that would cause such a discoloration. He also felt the roughness of the man's skin within the grip of the handshake. *Must be from working with his hands all day.*

"My name is Dr. Hudson Klemens," the custodian mimicked the doctor's proper voice and speech. His grip on the doctor's hand tightened to the point of pain, and Dr. Klemens noticed the coldness of the man's hand wrapped fully around his own, like he had just reached into a cooler full of ice.

"Okay? I really should be leaving now," Dr. Klemens trembled. The grip tightened more and forced his own hand into a fist. The sweat that formed in his palm felt slippery against his fingertips.

"I need you tonight, doc," the custodian returned to his normal baritone voice. "I wish I could trust you for a favor, but I'll just take you for myself."

Dr. Klemens tensed up and no longer felt the death grip that crushed his hand. The garage began to spin around in his mind as he fell back towards his car.

He caught himself on the trunk, but felt all sense of feeling and control flee away.

"Please," he mumbled. "Pleeease. I do wha' you need." Basic motor skills vanished as the doctor lay on his car. He leaned his head down and stared empty-mindedly at the elevator doors. He heard a loud, howling laugh through his muffled senses. Arms grasped around his neck and clenched tight.

The pressure gradually increased and the world turned black. The howl echoed within his mind as he slipped into another dimension where darkness gave way to a blinding whiteness that seemed never ending.

The custodian kept grinning as he lifted the doctor's limp body and dropped it into the back seat of the Mercedes.

"We have work to do, Dr. Klemens," he said in the doctor's tone. "We have a special patient on the way and need to take great care of him!"

He sat in the backseat on top of the doctor's legs and grabbed his limp arm towards his own face. The custodian inhaled to smell the doctor's hand and cracked a smile as he did.

"Too perfect," he whispered to himself in the silence of the car. He slid the doctor's hand into his mouth and clamped his dirty teeth around the flesh between the thumb and forefinger.

His jaw clenched as tightly as it allowed, drawing blood to the surface. He slurped blood from the hand and licked his lips in a gesture of appreciation.

Drowsiness kicked in almost instantly and he started to doze off, so he crawled to the front seat of the car and reclined the driver's seat to lay down. He would dispose of the doctor's dead body shortly, but first needed to go through a transformation. His hands crossed on his lap as he fell into a deep sleep.

His nap would be brief, and when he awoke, he would be Dr.

Hudson Klemens in the flesh. His special patient would arrive soon, and he had every intention on tending to him and his mother to get the job done he had set out to do.

9

Light snow fell above the hospital, something Travis hadn't noticed as he pulled up to the emergency room entrance. He killed the engine and jumped out of the driver's seat.

The boys had sat in silence for the remainder of the drive after Brian had explained his horrific story. Shock, concern, and doubt all mixed among the boys and Travis as they tried to grasp the reality of the events.

Travis could only wonder. The last time he discussed his mother's job with her, she assured him safety for the rest of his life. He never could get much detail from her on what to expect, but one thing he did know was that these people she hunted had gray skin. Once Brian mentioned gray skin, Travis let his mind roam and panic. He should have called her, but he called Brian's mother, Lauren, instead. Her son was headed to the emergency room after all, so the call to his own mother would have to wait.

The boys met him on the opposite side of the truck as they started to help Brian out of the backseat. He placed an arm around Kyle and another around Jimmy as he boosted himself up out of the truck.

Brian hobbled on one leg with his two human crutches supporting him towards the entrance. The automatic doors slid open as the boys approached and they welcomed the rush of warm air that smacked them across their faces.

A young nurse jumped up from behind the reception desk to help, bringing with her a wheelchair for Brian. Her blonde hair hung over her face as she looked down to adjust the wheelchair for Brian's size.

"Here you go," her soft voice welcomed. She looked up with a gentle smile as she brushed her hair back to reveal a sincere complexion.

Brian blushed as he looked into her sky blue eyes. Kyle giggled from behind as Brian unconsciously seated himself in the wheelchair.

"Let's get you signed in," the nurse said, acknowledging Brian's embarrassment. "What is your name?"

"Brian. . . Brian Carsner," his eyes remained entranced.

"It's nice to meet you, Brian," she said as she pushed his wheelchair to the registration desk. "My name is Jennifer. Do you have a parent with you?"

"My friend's dad, he's here," Brian finally regained some self-control. The chaos of the emergency room overwhelmed Brian as doctors seemed to sprint by with clipboards, phones rang off the hook, and nurses jumped over each other to answer them. A baby in the waiting area screamed his head off as an exhausted and distraught mother rocked him in her embrace, helplessly trying to sooth him.

"I'm here," Travis declared as he entered. "His mother is nearby and has the insurance for you. Are you still able to see him?"

"Yes, of course," Jennifer responded in a more professional tone than before. "We're extremely slammed this evening so it may be a few minutes. We'll call you back once a doctor is available."

"But his leg is cut wide open!" Travis snapped back.

"I know, sir, but the worst of the pain has seemed to fade. Blood loss is not near a dangerous level either," Jennifer explained calmly as if she had done it hundreds of times. "Please have a seat in the waiting area and I'll do all I can."

Travis shook his head in disappointment and turned towards the waiting room. Kyle pushed Brian in the wheelchair while the others followed. They all filled a row of vacant seats with Brian positioned in the aisle a couple feet across from Kyle.

"Look, boys," Travis stood up and perched one foot on the chair. "I don't know what's going on. The news mentioned a gray person and so did Brian. I'm not sure what to think any more these days with all the crazies in this world, but I think we should *not* mention anything about gray people. It can cause a panic and possibly bring us publicity we don't wanna deal with."

Travis knew his mother would have answers. He also knew a custody battle awaited him in court, and any story regarding gray people attacking kids under his watch was sure to project him as a total nut job in the eyes of the law.

The boys sat in silence as no one knew what to say. Brian looked down at his crossed hands on his lap while Mikey stared into space from his end of the row.

"Oh my God!" Lauren Carsner shrieked from the entrance. They all looked up from their daze to find Brian's mom standing in the sliding doors with her hands clapped to her face.

All five feet of her darted towards Brian, arms flailing until they wrapped around her son's shoulders. "What happened?" she demanded with a mixture of anger, fear, and concern in her voice.

"I'm fine, Mom," Brian said, keeping his voice uninterested.

"I was running through the woods and tripped and fell on a tree stump. It cut my leg, but it's just sore now."

Travis peered around to get a read on the others' reactions to Brian's lie. Kyle stared into the ground, Mikey watched the television showing an edited version of American Pie, and Jimmy stared straight ahead, stiff-necked, and lips pursed so tight they changed to a whitish tint.

"Well that's stupid of you," Lauren said and flicked Brian on top of his head. Travis let out an internal sigh of relief as Lauren bought it and the silent acceptance across the boys to keep the gray men talk to a minimum.

Travis maintained his stare on Lauren. He always had an attraction for her that he kept suppressed for obvious reasons, but now that he would soon be back on the market, he considered the possibilities. Lauren's estranged husband had walked out on her and Brian years ago, before him and Kyle had even met.

Why she remained single after so much time was beyond his understanding, but he would love to take the gamble and find out for himself. As one of the few mothers to keep a stunning and curvy figure deep into motherhood, the fathers always seemed to crowd around her at school functions.

Travis never participated in such adolescent behavior, but he also had the luxury of knowing Lauren on a more personal level thanks to Kyle and Brian's friendship (and her living across the street).

She stepped back from Brian and ignored Travis gawking at her tight yoga pants.

"Thanks for handling all of this, Travis." Her tone changed to appreciative.

"Not a problem, I'm sorry this happened," he responded

with a half smile.

"Brian!" nurse Jennifer shouted from the doorway that led into the hospital ward. She grinned gently as she hugged a clipboard against her chest.

"Okay, let's go, Tarzan," Lauren said as she pushed the wheelchair towards the nurse.

"We'll wait here for you guys," Travis said as they walked away.

"Follow me please," Jennifer said, radiating a giddy type of energy. They crossed into the main ward and passed a stone-faced security officer standing guard at the entrance. "You are in *great* hands today," she continued as they entered a room halfway down the never-ending hallway. "Since we have been so busy, some doctors have come down to help, and our very own Dr. Klemens is here and he'll get you all fixed up!"

Brian and Lauren stared blankly at the nurse and she could see their resemblance as clear as day, but they obviously did not understand Jennifer's enthusiasm.

"Dr. Klemens is one of the top surgeons and doctors in the country," she explained. "He's kind of a celebrity around here. And quite dreamy, Mrs. Carsner, you'll see."

It's Miss *Carsner,* Lauren snapped in her thoughts. It was an honest mistake for a stranger to make, so she decided to let it slide this time.

"Well, that's great news!" Lauren faked some excitement to avoid more awkwardness.

"Indeed it is," Jennifer refocused. "I need to check your vitals first. Do you know your blood type in case the doctor decides you need some? That's a pretty deep gash."

Brian looked at his mother in need of an answer as he had no clue what type of blood pumped through his veins. "He's A positive," Lauren informed both of them.

"Perfect." Jennifer worked quickly as she had already checked Brian's temperature and unstrapped the blood pressure cuff from around his arm. "Everything looks good. I'll send Dr. Klemens in."

"Thanks, Jennifer," Lauren said as the nurse dashed out of the room like a squirrel crossing the street. "She was cute don't you think?" Lauren asked Brian. She never held anything back with him. Brian blushed, causing a giggle from his mother. "So how is your pain?"

"It's fine, just sore." He stared down at the parted skin on his thigh. "They took care of me on the drive up."

"That's good." Lauren rubbed her eyes. "How is Travis? I know he's dealing with a lot right now."

"He seemed alright, I guess. A little quieter than usual, but he seemed to enjoy himself this weekend."

Lauren would be in denial if she didn't admit to being slightly intrigued by Travis. His attraction to her was reciprocated as long as they knew each other. The situation could get sticky with their kids' friendship as she had to consider what the other parents would say if things developed into something serious. How would she explain to Brian? Or her neighbor and Travis's soon-to-be ex-wife? They already had a good friendship in place and this could potentially put an end even to that. *Never too old for friends with benefits, I suppose.* All of the stress of the possibilities dampered her desires. It almost seemed not worth it. Almost.

A rapid knock rapped on the door, disrupting her thoughts as a handsome doctor entered the room.

"Brian?" he asked. "I'm Dr. Klemens. Nice to meet you." The doctor held out a firm hand.

"Hi Doc, nice meeting you as well," Brian responded and returned the shake.

"And I take it you are Mom?" He turned his attention to Lauren. A slight red flushed her cheeks and this time Brian chuckled under his breath.

"Yes. Lauren. I've heard so much about you," she said anxiously and shook his hand.

"Well, nice meeting you both," Dr. Klemens continued. "Now I see we have quite the wound here. What happened?"

Wow, he is dreamy, Lauren let her mind wander while Brian explained his story again. *His smile is perfect, almost looks fake.*

"Mom?" Brian called out. Lauren had fallen into some sort of hypnosis and the conversation drowned into the background. She snapped out of her trance and rejoined the party.

"I'm so sorry, I'm out in La-La Land," she replied as the two stared at her. Dr. Klemens shot her a sly grin.

"Mom, he said I need a blood transfusion."

"Yes, Ms. Carsner," the doctor explained. "I don't like where your son's blood pressure currently sits to send you home quite yet. It's nothing to be concerned about, but I think a small amount of blood will help clear things up. We can have you out of here in an hour."

Brian turned pale from the news. A blood transfusion sounded plenty serious to him.

"It's okay, Bry, it's a common procedure," Lauren comforted him. She had done some administrative work at the hospital downtown and saw plenty of blood transfusions processed every day.

"Yes, in fact, one of the most common procedures done, just like getting a shot," Dr. Klemens chimed in. "I've already done three of them today!"

Brian stared down at his twiddling thumbs as if he had no control over them. Dr. Klemens and Lauren observed and exchanged smiles.

"Alright, let's get it over with," Brian said as if defeated.

"Terrific, let's head on up," the doctor responded with an odd excitement. "We'll need to borrow a room with a bed and machines to monitor your vitals. And don't worry Ms. Carsner, the room won't be billed to you, we're just borrowing it."

As if he read her mind, she nodded in acknowledgement, thinking that none of this sounded like the protocol in a hospital, but maybe when you are a hot shot doctor you can get away with whatever you want.

"You'll take the elevator down the hall up to the fifth floor. I'll have Jennifer meet you up there," Dr. Klemens instructed. "I need to gather some paperwork and I'll see you in five minutes." He opened the door and extended an arm to allow Lauren and Brian to exit.

"Thank you, doctor," Lauren said as she stood up and took her post behind the wheelchair. "About an hour you said?"

"Yes ma'am." He grinned awkwardly.

Lauren rolled Brian into the hallway and turned towards the elevator. The lighting in hospitals always made her head throb and this time was no different.

"Mom, what was that?" Brian looked over his shoulder to catch a glimpse of his mother.

"What do you mean?" she asked.

"Umm, the doctor!" Brian gasped. "I'm pretty sure you were drooling over him in there."

"Well, hey, he's a sexy man. What else can I say?" Lauren blushed again. She had an open door policy with Brian regarding her love life. He wanted her to be happy and move past the traumatic abandonment by his father. Because of this, conversations about potential men came across casually for Brian and led him to poking fun at his mother if she made a fool of herself, as she did with Dr. Klemens.

They pulled up to the elevator and Brian leaned forward to push the call button.

"Maybe I'll ask the doctor for his business card, just in case," Lauren grinned.

"Oh Mom, don't be so desperate," Brian sighed in response. "We talked about playing hard to get."

Well, I'm not getting any younger, she thought as the elevator doors parted ways.

An elderly man waddled out of the elevator and winked at Brian. A baggy, leather Denver Broncos jacket draped loosely over his thin frame. Brian noticed the multiple teeth missing from his grin, but still felt his genuineness shining through.

Lauren pushed Brian into the vacant elevator and turned him around to face the door. "Fifth floor," she told him as he was positioned in front of the panel. He pushed the 5 and watched the old man exit through the lobby doors as the elevator closed.

Brian remained consumed with the thought of his dad out in the world somewhere. Could the older man have been his own grandfather? He would never know as Lauren refused to speak of her former in-laws. He knew they lived out of state and only came to Colorado for their wedding. Their names and appearance remained a mystery.

The elevator gave its welcoming chime as the doors parted on the fifth floor. Brian was thrust into the small lobby of this floor, snapping him out of his thoughts. His new crush, Jennifer, greeted them with her clipboard back in hand.

"Please follow me," she gestured with a wave of the arm.

They followed her into a hospital room with a bed made to perfection. Jennifer stood in the corner and typed away on a computer.

"Go ahead and lie down and we can get your IV set up," she said, not breaking her concentration from the monitor. "Dr. Klemens should be right in."

Brian rose from the wheelchair, keeping all his body weight on his good leg, and limped a couple steps towards the bed, sprawling across it in relief.

Jennifer strode towards the door to close it while she snapped on a pair of white rubber gloves.

"Alright," she announced as Lauren took a seat in the recliner on the far side of the room. "Let's get you ready."

She explained the process as she strapped on a blood pressure cuff and clipped a finger pulse oximeter onto his forefinger.

"Now the important one," she explained and pulled out a small needle. "This will go just below the inside of your elbow. It'll be a small prick at first, but no pain as long as you don't fling your arm around."

She wiped the area with a swab of rubbing alcohol that left its stench in the air for several minutes. Brian held in his cringe as she inserted the IV needle into his arm and taped it down to his flesh. Her hair dropped down in front of Brian's face as she situated the needle and he caught a whiff of her fruity shampoo, a new scent he had grown fond of lately.

A double knock rapped on the door followed by Dr. Klemens storming into the room.

"Are we ready?" Dr. Klemens asked.

"Everything is set, Doctor," Jennifer responded and took a step back.

Dr. Klemens held a small blood bag in his hand that hung to

his side. The blood looked almost black to Brian rather than the red shade he had expected, causing a nauseous feeling to spread through his gut.

"Let me know if you need anything while you're here," Jennifer said, giving Brian a soft pat on the arm.

"Thank you," Lauren responded from her post in the recliner. Jennifer departed and Dr. Klemens approached Brian.

"Cute girl, don'tcha think?" he asked in a tone eerily like his mother's. His cheeks flushed once again and the doctor recognized his embarrassment. "Let's begin, shall we?"

Dr. Klemens hooked the blood bag to the IV pole and connected the tubing from Brian's arm to the adjoining end. The tube changed from clear to the black looking color as blood rushed through.

"And that's all it is," Dr. Klemens cheered. "You can move around if you want; just roll this pole with you. Give it an hour and I'll come back to check on you. Anything I can get for either of you?"

Brian shook his head as he tried to fight of the woozy feeling taking over.

"Dinner next weekend?" Lauren asked from her seat.

"Mom!" Brian exclaimed and sat upright, forgetting all about the wooziness.

"I'd love that," Dr. Klemens said with a tight grin. "I'll leave you my card before you take off."

"Sounds like a date, Doc," Lauren smiled back.

Brian looked back and forth between the two in complete shock. Dr. Klemens shuffled out of the room and closed the door behind him.

"Mom!" Brian raised his voice again. "What *was* that?" His jaw hung open, still unable to believe the last few seconds of events.

"What?" she played dumb. "I can't ask a doctor on a date?"

"Not here, not like this," Brian snapped. "He's helping me."

"Who cares? Things happen for a reason. People come in and out of your life whether you like it or not." Lauren used her don't-question-your-mother tone and Brian knew better than to continue the argument.

He laid back down and dreaded the hour he had to kill. Thoughts popped in and out of his mind. He wondered what could have provoked his father to leave behind an infant son. Was it something his mother did? Did he have his own demons in life that he couldn't handle? Brian had tried numerous times to pry this information from his mom, but she refused to discuss the matter, always saying there would be a "right time" for explanations.

He had learned at a young age that sometimes people live with dark secrets in their heart to protect others around them, and usually those secrets remained with that person all the way to the grave. He had heard stories of men leaving their families to start a whole new life elsewhere with a new wife and new children, as if the previous life never even existed. Perhaps Lauren knew of this and couldn't bring herself to discuss it.

At the end of the day, Brian needed to remind himself that his mother had to cope with the same issue and she dealt with it in her own way. If that meant asking strange doctors to dinner, then so be it.

As if he could hear his thoughts at that moment, Dr. Klemens knocked and let himself in.

"Should be all set, Brian," he said with a charming grin. Brian checked the clock next to the door and was surprised to find the hour had passed during his Q and A session with himself.

His mother had fallen asleep in the recliner and stretched her arms as she awoke.

"Good morning to you, Ms. Carsner. I hope you like eggs and bacon for breakfast." Dr. Klemens winked at her.

Oh hell no! Brian thought, grossed out.

"Mmhmm," she moaned at the peak of her stretch. Her blouse raised enough to show her navel and Brian caught the doctor staring.

This is fucked up. Brian cleared his throat to create a diversion.

"Well then," Dr. Klemens returned his attention to Brian. "Let's check your pulse and blood pressure and get you guys out of here."

He pressed buttons on the computer behind the IV pole and they beeped back in response. Brian felt a little lightheaded but thought nothing of it as his exhaustion from the day continued to grow like a bad fungus on his mind.

"Looks like your body responded fine to the blood," Dr. Klemens explained. He tore the cuff off Brian's arm, allowing the blood to rush back to his fingertips, causing a tingling sensation. "You're set to leave."

Brian sat up and dangled his legs over the side of the bed before lowering himself. "What about my leg? Shouldn't I get stitches or something?"

"Your leg will recover fine," Dr. Klemens responded as he helped Brian gain his footing. "No stitches needed. Just keep it wrapped and clean as you have, and always elevate it when you can. It'll be a couple days until you can put full pressure on it, but that wound will heal no matter how ugly it may look."

"Thank you, Dr. Klemens." Lauren approached the bed.

"My pleasure, Ms. Carsner," he replied and pulled a business card from the front pocket of his lab coat. "Here's my card as promised. I look forward to next weekend."

"I'll see you then." Lauren snatched the card from his grip. "Do I need to sign us out or anything?"

"No, you're all set. Everything is taken care of."

Sounds wrong again. I haven't filled out any paperwork since being here and I'm leaving with a stranger's blood in my son's arm. No info, no bill I suppose.

"Alright let's get out of here, mister." Lauren helped Brian limp out of the room as he insisted he no longer needed the wheelchair. "Thanks again, Doctor."

Dr. Klemens waved them out as they proceeded down the hall one limp at a time.

Once they entered the elevator, Brian felt that lightheaded sensation take over again. He leaned on the back wall for support while the elevator descended. It felt like his brain was spinning on an axis even though he remained still. Breakfast was the last meal he had eaten, and the evening at the hospital carried him well past a regular dinnertime. He didn't *feel* hungry, but it seemed to be a logical explanation for his state of mind.

"Hello?" Lauren nudged him and gave a puzzled look. "I asked if you wanna grab dinner on the way home? Maybe stop at The Burrito House and get some nachos to take home?"

"Yeah, sorry." Brian regained some of his focus. "I really wanna lay down. I feel so tired, but that sounds good right now too."

"I know. We'll get food and you can even eat it in bed if you want. Just for tonight."

They reached the ground level and stepped out to find Travis and the boys sitting as they had left them. *American Pie* gave way to *The Sandlot* and Travis watched with much interest as

Wendy Peffercorn rescued a faking Squints. Kyle had fallen asleep, head dangling downward into his chest, while Jimmy sat silently next to him. Mikey typed away on his laptop with headphones over his ears, likely playing a video game.

Brian limped over to them with the dizziness coming in waves.

"Hey guys, we can leave now!" he called out. They all jerked out of their trances except for Kyle who remained asleep. Travis stood up.

"Are you okay?" he asked.

"He's going to be fine," Lauren answered for him. "He'll be limping for a few days, but no stitches needed, apparently."

"Glad to hear." Travis patted Brian on the shoulder. "We're going to eat if you guys wanna join us."

"Thanks, Mr. W, but I really want to get home. I'm not feeling so hot." The boys had formed a semicircle around him; Kyle woke in a daze and strolled over like a zombie.

"I understand," Travis said. "Go rest up and I'll probably see you both at the party later this week."

"See you guys later. Thanks for everything today," Brian said to his friends.

They each stepped in and gave him the teenage version of a friend hug with a quick slap on his back. Tired and drained from the events of the day, they all walked out at a much slower pace than usual.

Even though nothing had been officially said earlier, they all pledged a silent oath to keep the truth about the gray man a secret among themselves.

10

"I don't believe this," Susan said to herself, trying to stay calm. She sat at the desk in her quiet office with her reading glasses rested on the bridge of her nose as she read an email from her laptop.

She had received a briefing report with the latest updates on the Exalls. A department within The Crew, called the Center of Intelligence (C.O.I.), maintained up-to-date status reports on all the information gathered about the Exall species. They constantly studied, tracked, and followed every Exall on the planet, even the ones considered "off limits" in other countries.

Their job was tedious by nature as they had to log every single action they witnessed by an Exall, no matter how big or small it seemed. The hard work had its benefits, however, as it resulted in a database of knowledge of their enemy species.

So many small details had been gathered over the years to create a clear, big picture of the Exalls' capabilities and motives. Their rapid advancements in technology over time were also considered by the C.O.I.

Susan remembered doing some work for this sect back in the early eighties. She found the work exciting for about a whole day before deciding it was too boring for her active mind. Boredom aside, she still helped mold the department into what it would remain for years to follow.

Her time in the C.O.I. was short lived as hundreds of fresh college graduates were recruited by the government after a mass expansion of the Crew, called for by President Reagan. The focus of The Crew shifted towards thorough research of the Exalls and less on combat training.

The Crew hired one hundred college graduates to cover every background possible. English majors worked with History majors and Biotechnology majors alike. In one of the few department-wide meetings, which all Crew members were required to attend, the President discussed the need to have "all hands on deck", and that the reason for having the various backgrounds on board was to provide different insight and points of view on the research and data that was gathered.

The meeting took place many levels below the Pentagon in a two-hour session led by the President. He gave a passionate speech on the survival of the human race and the Crew's role in preserving that life. Everyone left the meeting fired up and ready to shoulder their load in ensuring the Exalls could never harm a single citizen again.

The energy trickled down from the President all the way to the C.O.I. team. They attacked their research like bloodhounds, working around the clock with a clear thirst for knowledge that grew with each revelation uncovered.

A banner hung in their section of the office that read, "AL-WAYS ASK WHY…THEN FIGURE IT OUT!" With this mantra in place, every answer led to another question in what turned out to be a never-ending cycle of deep diving into various matters.

All the knowledge led to the present day with Susan's jaw dropped in shock as she read the newest updates. She hadn't kept up in almost five years as they were typically long lists of data that rambled on for pages about nothing significant.

Now as she prepared for a battle, the latest updates frightened her to the bone. The key points were summarized at the top of the report:

-Ability to transform into a human through consumption of human blood

-Ability to control humans via injection of Exall blood into the human

-Capable of reading human thoughts

-Ability to influence the human mind

-Capable of driving vehicles

Susan felt so far out of the loop. Never in her wildest nightmare could an Exall drive a car, turn into a human, *and* control her very mind. Their advancement grew so rapidly and drastically that she felt uncertainty start to creep in as she thought forward to the impending war.

How could she be expected to fight off a species that had advanced light years ahead of her own world's amazing technology? If they could read minds, that eliminated any chance of a surprise attack on unsuspecting Exalls.

"What in Christ's name can I do?" she whispered. "I can't plan anything if they know it's coming."

She removed her glasses and rubbed her eyes in frustration. Crew members were set to fly into Denver the next day and a meeting was already planned to discuss a plan of attack.

"Guess we're wingin' it," she said as she slammed her laptop shut. Not once had she felt so helpless during her time with The Crew.

She left the office and sat on her bed in the adjoining bedroom. An email she had started writing earlier on her phone remained unfinished, so she returned to typing. The message provided a schedule for the five Crew members set to land within the next couple of days with meeting times and locations outlined.

Susan attached the briefing she just read to the message along with each Crew member's profile. When carrying out these missions, it was rare to work with someone you already knew, so she liked to provide some background on each team member.

Day one always consisted of a team bonding and trust building activity. Their time together was limited, but they would also be relying on each other to protect their lives. The objective was to get to know everyone on a personal level, but having a room full of people who are forbidden to talk about their job with their friends and family always directed the conversation back to exactly that.

Susan didn't mind, as she understood the stress and tension that built up as a result of the type of work they did. Without some sort of release every now and then among peers, people could start to slowly die from the inside, which she had seen plenty of times.

She concluded the email, pressed *SEND*, and lay back on to the bed. Two pictures of Jesus and Mary watched over her from the head of the bed as she fell asleep.

* * * * *

The day gave way to nighttime before she awoke. Little did she know that two blocks down, the boys had arrived home from a troubling evening at the hospital. Brian went to bed feeling as sick as ever, clueless that the blood injected into his system was not quite human.

They had the fortune of all residing on the same block, a helpful component in maintaining their strong friendships. The neighborhood had an eerie silence as a couple of crickets chirped away in the night. The snow hadn't made its way down the mountain so the city remained warm.

A streetlight posted on the corner of the front lawn shone its light onto the Wells home like a dim spotlight while the boys poured out of the truck. Brian lived across the street and they could all see Lauren's car parked in the driveway and the glow of lights through their main living room window.

They retrieved all their bags from the truck and helped unload everything else. Fist bumps and half hugs went around the circle of friends as Mikey and Jimmy split away with their backpacks slung over their shoulders.

"See you guys in paradise tomorrow!" Mikey said as he walked away.

School awaited them in the morning with a long week ahead. The boys basketball team, which included all four of them, had won their district's basketball championship and had a school-wide banquet planned for Friday to cap off the week.

Classes were even scheduled around a half day so the banquet could begin at noon. Larkwood Middle School took its sports programs seriously, and the over-the-top celebration for middle school basketball proved that.

These kids enjoyed the royal treatment since they hoisted the trophy two weeks earlier when their principal, an ex-Olympian, delivered a passionate victory speech in front of all the students in a cramped gymnasium. Kyle enjoyed the victory as it fueled his competitive spirit, but he couldn't give two shits about all the fluff that came with it afterwards.

After his mother volunteered their home to the team, parents, and eighth grade class for an after party to follow, an argument sparked between his parents that snowballed out of control. Kyle didn't want all of his schoolmates over either, but decided to not press the matter any further and gave in to his mom's wishes.

Kyle was even entertained in the preparation for the party, getting into debates over party decorations and the classic battle of pizza versus a six-foot sub sandwich. Travis joined them, and for the first time in a while, his mom and dad laughed together and seemed to enjoy each other's company.

Little did Kyle know the joy he witnessed could be attributed to them finalizing their divorce that very day, taking a huge load off their shoulders. All paperwork was signed and placed in the mailbox. They agreed to not break the news to Kyle until the school year ended, and also to give Travis some time to find a place to live.

The party at their house would likely be their last event together as a family and they wanted to make the best of it for themselves and Kyle.

11

Travis had called his mother on Monday morning, wasting no time in demanding information about the suspicious activity he had witnessed. She had always filled him in on stories as a teen and young adult about the species she fought off in her prime. He could also do the simple math and connect the dots that all these years later, these same beings were back as expected, and ready to raise hell.

"Yes, Travis, it's them," she told him. "You have nothing to worry about anymore. They're after me and were just trying to send me a scare through you."

His story about them following them through the mountains didn't surprise her. She knew the type of twisted people the Exalls were and expected nothing less.

"Just stay alert, and we'll discuss it at the party Friday," she said. "I'll fill you in on everything."

Travis took the words to heart, knowing his mother never misguided him about her work. She had always been upfront with him about the dangers of her profession, and he knew if she said he was safe, she meant it. The week dragged along as he anxiously awaited the upcoming news, anticipating it to be much worse than it seemed based on how busy his mother seemed during the week.

For the boys, the school week passed in a blur, bringing on

Friday and the big banquet planned for the boys basketball team later that afternoon. They had sneaked away during their afternoon recess early in the week, wanting to discuss the events of the weekend, but weren't able to force the issue. An awkward tension hung over them to keep quiet surrounding the matter, afraid that someone might over hear them and think they were all nutcases.

Kyle's Friday started out like any other school day with his radio alarm blaring throughout his room as its clock read *7:00 a.m.*, and the annoying sound of Justin Bieber vomited out of the speakers.

He groaned and swung his arm to slam the snooze button, cutting off Justin from telling his baby to go and love herself. The mornings and Kyle had a mutual agreement to not get along. No matter what time he fell asleep, seven in the morning was too damn early to be awake.

He laid in bed and stared at the ceiling through groggy eyes. The sunshine filled his east facing bedroom with its usual chipper attitude, further motivating his petition to relocate into the basement. "Maybe in high school" was the typical response when the question was asked. *Well, high school is right around the corner!*

"Rise and shine!" Kyle's mother barged into the room. As part of their morning ritual, she needed to make sure he got out of bed.

Lori Wells had always enjoyed the mornings, so it seemed natural for Kyle to find her annoying at that time of day. She owned and operated the local Italian restaurant in town named *Dolce Ragazzo,* which translated to "Sweet Boy".

Even though Kyle acted nothing like a sweet boy in the mornings, she knew the big heart he possessed. The restaurant lifestyle came with grueling hours, leaving Kyle puzzled as to how his mother could exude so much energy at the crack of dawn.

"Don't make me pull you out of that bed, young man," she commanded as she leaned against the door frame with a smirk on her face.

Kyle rolled out of bed, hitting the ground with a hard thump. He saw his mother already dressed for the day in her jeans and button up *Dolce Ragazzo* polo. Her hair hung down to her shoulders and was a light enough shade of blonde to hide the streaks of white that had started to appear.

Kyle's hair stood up in a crazy mess after a rough night's sleep. He dreamed of being chased through the woods by the gray men in the Ford Explorer. Every time he closed his eyes he could see them vividly in his mind, flipping them off and howling like hyenas.

Perhaps the banquet and after party would help take his mind off of them for a while. All week in school the boys would gather in private during their free time and try to discuss the happenings of the weekend, but decided they shouldn't until they could find out more from Travis.

Brian's wound healed and left nothing but a minor scar to commemorate his experience. His limp became subtle, but he expected that to disappear in the coming days. They agreed to continue the lie to their classmates that he had tripped on to a tree stump. No one doubted the story as Brian had the reputation as the class klutz.

"Okay, I'm up," Kyle whined. "Let me get ready."

"Alright," Lori responded. "Big day of parties today, champ." She winked and left his room.

I'm so sick of hearing about this ridiculous party.

Kyle proceeded to get ready for the day, putting on his basketball warmups as the team was asked to match for the banquet. He met his mother in the kitchen for a quick bowl of cereal, grabbed his backpack, and was out the door within minutes.

"Have a good morning, and I'll see you later!" Lori called out.

"You too. Love you," Kyle said as he closed the door behind him. His school was a quick, four block walk from his house. He usually met with Brian to walk together, but he was still too slow to make the hike. Friday marked the fifth day of walking to school by himself and he found the peacefulness quite enjoyable.

Snow may have pounded the mountains, but the spring mornings in the city brought only a slight chill. Once the sun made its way through the clouds, the temperature was perfect in Kyle's opinion. A frosty dew covered the lawns he passed and the only sounds came from high in the trees from birds singing their morning tunes. An occasional car drove by, but he remained oblivious as he thought about the day ahead.

His excitement grew for the banquet. They did win a championship after all, and there was no discounting the hours of hard work the team put in to perfect their coach's game plan.

The pace of his steps increased as he arrived to a downhill slope, which marked one more block to the school. Its brick exterior became visible along with the large sign smacked across the front that read *LARKWOOD MIDDLE SCHOOL*. He crossed the final street and set foot on the school's baseball field that marked the official school grounds, and noticed the school's adjoining parking lot had more cars than usual. Other vehicles pulled up to the shrubbery in front of the main entrance and kids jumped out to race towards the building.

Kyle felt an upbeat energy radiating from the school as he approached, and didn't believe it was due to the pending celebration. The morning was the warmest of the year. Kids wore their shorts and skirts, tricking their minds into summer vacation mode. Nothing like some sunshine in March to make everyone giddy arriving at school, despite knowing a thunderstorm was forecasted for later in the day.

Kyle approached the wide steps that led into the school and walked up to the heavy blue doors. Another student, likely a sixth grader judging from his size, held the door open for him. He thanked him and the kid's face lit up revealing his crooked teeth and fresh braces.

While he passed other classrooms in the hall, he could hear the energy pouring out of the rooms. Loud chatter and laughter filled the air along with some stomping from the second floor above their heads. Kyle reached his destination at the end of the hall and entered Mr. Swirsky's classroom.

Mr. Swirsky was a favorite among his students, as he was known as a laid back teacher. Few things bothered him, but tardiness was one crime that shouldn't be committed under his watch. The door remained open until the bell rang, and if someone had to open the door to enter, they were considered late and lost ten minutes of recess time. "Being punctual is the first step to success," he often preached when a straggler came in late, usually panting.

Kyle glanced at the large clock that hung in the hallway and felt relieved to see 7:58. He walked through the open door into a mob of his classmates carrying on their morning conversations. He was last to arrive as he found his desk, located on the front row against the window, as the only vacant one.

"What's up, bro?" Kyle asked Mikey, seated behind him.

"Ready for the weekend, and ready to party!"

"I hear that," Kyle responded as the bell rang.

Mr. Swirsky always entered the room as the bell rang; today was no exception. "Good morning class, and happy Friday." He placed his worn, leather briefcase across his desk.

He wore a suit like any other day, never afraid to take chances with some flashy color schemes, with sky blue pants that led to a gray plaid suit jacket with a complementing red and blue plaid shirt underneath. "You never know who you'll meet on any given day," he explained for his attire. The only time you would find him not in a suit was during baseball season. He coached the school's team and couldn't quite commit to keeping the suit on in the dugout, like Connie Mack back in the day.

Ryan Swirsky had just turned thirty-three and moved to Colorado from Indiana. He majored in English and found his job at the local newspaper not as fulfilling as expected. His passion turned to writing books and short stories, so he took the first job he could find as an English teacher.

His first book idea would discuss the uncertainty that writers deal with on a daily basis. In his opinion, the writing industry seemed to not be taken seriously and a lack of appreciation for the craft was clear from his time at the newspaper.

Teaching provided three things for Ryan: the sharpening of his grammar skills, the hope of molding some future writers, and most importantly, three months off every summer to buckle down and complete his book. The first two proved to be true. He made writing and learning fun for his students, and they engaged in classroom discussion as a result. It was an instance where the teacher got as much out of the class as his students.

Summer break awaited a tempting six weeks away. He had

written the first fifty pages of his book over the course of the school year and would will himself to the finish line during summer. Dreams of a published book that might pay the bills no longer seemed like such a far-fetched fantasy.

Before any dreams came true, though, he needed to teach his class. Class times were shortened to the point of uselessness, and none of his students seemed to have any sense of concentration as a result.

He scrapped the lesson on building bibliographies and turned the floor over to the kids for their current reading of *The Diary of Anne Frank.* With only half an hour to spare it seemed a more logical choice then attempting to introduce a new concept.

His attempt at a lively discussion failed as half the class hadn't read their assignments, and the other half had already mentally checked out for the day. "Everyone enjoy the festivities today, and congrats to the boys again on a great season," he said as the bell gave its cue to release his restless prisoners of education.

Mr. Swirsky didn't give a shit how well the basketball team performed, as long as none of his baseball players injured themselves on the court. No other sport compared to baseball for him. He even went as far to say that baseball was, in fact, the only actual sport, while all others were nothing more than silly games.

Besides, the basketball coach, Mr. Ostrom (also the math teacher), was a dick. Mr. Swirsky avoided encounters with him at all costs. His disdain stemmed from their first conversation after he joined the staff where Mr. Ostrom made a statement regarding no athletic skill being necessary to play baseball. Being the new guy, Mr. Swirsky bit his lip and muddled his way through occasional small talk, wishing to get him on a baseball field and show him the truth.

He dreaded the upcoming banquet, knowing Mr. Ostrom would deliver a speech about how great his team was along with some self-proclaiming statements about his talents as a coach. Cocky bastard. The motivational quote posters stared at Mr. Swirsky as he stood at his ratty old desk. "Dare to be Different" headlined a poster of a single orange surrounded by hundreds of apples.

Who comes up with this shit? he wondered as he waited for his next class to start filing in.

* * * * *

The remainder of the morning dragged by, at least for Mr. Swirsky. To the students, their rather effortless day zipped by with ease. The final bell rang at noon and middle schoolers flooded the hallways like the breaking of a dam.

All students needed to arrive at the gymnasium within ten minutes. The banquet would commence at exactly 12:15 according to the announcement issued over the school's intercom system.

Kyle fought his way down the hallway through herds of classmates. He had departed from his advanced mathematics class on the second floor, the only class where none of his friends joined him.

A log jam of rowdy students caused delays on the only stairwell in the building. He could see Jimmy and Mikey at the bottom of the stairs as they entered the gymnasium.

The two girls in front of him, Vanessa and Mandy, whispered to each other, likely gossiping about anything they could.

Kyle got along with most of his classmates, though not as

much as his tight circle of friends. Vanessa, however, rubbed him the wrong way. Gossip aside, he felt a sense of distrust in her presence. She had a shrilling laugh that rang in his head like a car alarm.

He could only see the back of her head as she continued to whisper and giggle with her friend. Her jet black hair was pulled back into a thick ponytail that swung back and forth with every head movement. Three steps seemed a safe distance to avoid getting sucked into a conversation with Mandy and her snake of a friend.

They reached the bottom landing of the stairwell, which opened up into the hallway that led to the gym, and the herd of cattle separated, allowing everyone to ease into the gym.

Through the doorway Kyle caught a glimpse of hundreds of blue and white streamers and balloons hanging from the ceiling.

When he entered the gym, the buzz of nearly one hundred people swarmed over him. Twenty round tables filled the space of the gym floor with blue tablecloths spread over each one. Families made small talk while Kyle scanned the room for his parents.

A podium stood at the front of the room and he found his family in the second row of tables, seated directly behind the table reserved for the basketball players. He saw an open seat next to where Brian sat. His grandmother waved at him as he sat down and shot a quick wave back to his smiling family.

Brian and Mikey bickered about the massive drape that hung on the wall above the podium with a thin white rope hanging down from it.

Mikey insisted a plaque hid beneath while Brian believed a banner would be unveiled. The school had never won a championship in any sport, so they had no basis to go off.

Numerous men and women in matching black attire sped walked around the room in a chaotic, yet organized manner. A catering service was hired by the school and with everyone seated, lunch needed to be served.

The black vested wait staff bolted out of the cafeteria where they had set up trays of covered, plated meals stacked upon one another.

Silverware clinked throughout the room as everyone received their meals of grilled chicken, mashed potatoes, and steamed veggies. The boys wasted no time attacking their dish and just about finished by the time the principal approached the podium with Mr. Ostrom behind him.

Victor Romano, principal of Larkwood Middle School, tapped his fingers on the microphone for a brief sound check. With Mr. Ostrom behind him, the two stood out like a couple of towers over looking the city.

Mr. Romano had competed in the 1984 Olympics for the United States men's wrestling team. Even in his mid-fifties, he maintained most of the bulk from his bronze medal glory days. Combine his muscle mass with a bald head and groomed goatee, and his presence could intimidate even Chuck Norris.

A group of students sitting in the back started a brief applause, and Mr. Romano raised both hands in the air with fingers that looked as large as bananas.

"Thank you all for joining us in our celebration today," he said in a thunderous voice as the applause tapered off. "Our school has long excelled in academics and high school prep. When I became principal eight years ago the only sport our school had was girl's volleyball.

"One of my top priorities was to expand our non-existent

athletic department, and today I am proud to say we have eight sports teams in total for our boys and girls to participate in."

More applause and some whistling followed this statement.

"Today I stand before you a humbled man. It is with great honor to introduce our school's very first championship title. Boys please stand and take a bow."

The team seated at the front two tables stood in unison to an eruption of cheers from their families and classmates. Some of the boys embraced the moment and waved out toward the full gym. Others stood with their hands in their pockets, unsure what to do.

"I would like to introduce the man who led these boys throughout their accomplished season," Mr. Romano continued. "Coach Greg Ostrom, come on up here!" Mr. Romano reached his arm back to welcome Mr. Ostrom to the podium as more applause echoed.

"Thank you, thank you!" Mr. Ostrom had to shout over the commotion. He pulled a piece of paper from his back pocket and unfolded it on the podium." I've never been one for public speaking," he continued in a stiff voice. "Uh, I want to start by thanking these great boys. You all put in so much work this year, and I'm glad you got to see the benefits of that work."

Mr. Ostrom continued in his monotone voice, reminiscing on certain memories from the season and thanked the parents for their equally hard work. His victory speech concluded with a promise to work even harder during the next season in the hopes of defending their title while the boys entered their journey into high school.

"Now the moment you have been waiting for," Mr. Ostrom said with a little more life in his voice. "I saw you boys looking at the drape on the wall. Behind the drape is a gift from myself,

Mr. Romano, and all of your parents. Mr. Romano will you please do the honors?"

Mr. Romano obliged with a grin and gave the dangling rope a strong tug.

Applause ruptured once again as the majority of families provided a standing ovation for the gift they donated.

A large banner was unveiled, about the size of two basketball backboards put together. A deep blue decorated the banner with white lettering that read "2016 District Champions, Boys Basketball". Below the text was the school's logo; a Knight in full body armor, holding a shield and sword.

The final touch, which Kyle noticed immediately, was each player's name in the same white text printed around the edge of the banner to create a complementing border.

"Hangin' banners baby!" Mikey shouted and gave Kyle a fist bump. "What's next? The White House to meet the President!"

Mikey loved professional sports, and the fact he was receiving a trophy and banner excited him beyond normal.

The boys on the team finished giving each other hugs as Mr. Romano approached the podium with the biggest smile any of the students had ever seen from their principal.

"Congratulations again, boys" he said, regaining his composure as a powerful public speaker. "Thank you to the staff for making this ceremony happen. Thank you to the parents for your continued support. And thank you to all the students, all the Knights, who make this an incredible experience to come here everyday. Let's keep doing great things and make the world a better place!"

Mr. Romano walked out of the back door with Mr. Swirsky as the final round of applause showered them. Some students and parents rose from their seats as a short, plump woman raced to the podium.

"Excuse me," she shouted into the mic with a gasp as she caught her breath. The chatter fell silent. "There will be additional snack and beverages served in the cafeteria in fifteen minutes. We look forward to seeing you there. Thank you."

The round woman was Anjelica Ortiz, the school's assistant principal and Mr. Romano's right hand. She led the organization of the ceremony and apparently Mr. Romano forgot to give the announcement at the end of his speech. She walked calmly back to her table along the side with the rest of the faculty.

Kyle left his teammates to join his family to hug his grandmother and thank her for coming.

"Wouldn't miss this for anything," she responded and squeezed him. "Excited for your party, too! Should be a good time."

Little did anyone know the hell she had dealt with earlier that morning as she put together the final touches on a mission to be carried out later that weekend.

Travis and Lori stood together next to Susan with big, fake grins on their faces.

God, they hide their hate so good in public.

"Good shit, son," Travis said as he smacked Kyle on the back. "Proud of all you boys."

"Pretty cool banner, huh?" Lori chimed in. Kyle smiled and nodded in agreement.

"Well, your mother and I need to get home to finish setting up the party," Travis explained. "Hang out with your friends and be home in an hour to welcome our guests."

"Sounds good," Kyle responded. "Grandma are you coming early or late?" Susan rarely stayed for an entire event. She either came to the first half or the last half. It didn't bother the family as they had become accustomed to it. She had a demanding job and they could only be thankful that she showed up at all.

"I'll be there on time, Ky," Susan answered. "I plan on staying all night. I'll need to make a couple calls at some point, but nothing that'll keep me long."

"Great! Then I guess I'll see you in a bit," Kyle said and hugged her farewell.

Travis and Lori started towards the exit and waved towards Kyle. The gym doors remained open all day to not overheat the big crowd. The blazing brightness of the outside world stared into the gym from its two parallel doors with silhouettes entering and exiting through these spaces, with Kyle's mother and father among them.

"Okay, Ky, I'll see you later," Susan said as she looked down at her cell phone. A couple of urgent emails came in from Colonel Griffins and she needed to follow up immediately.

Kyle departed his grandmother as she drifted towards the hallway conjoining the gym to the school. He chuckled as he had never seen someone her age walk and text as smoothly as her. She looked like the rest of the middle school kids, glued to their hand held screens, oblivious to the world right in front of them. Brian stood in the doorway to the cafeteria and carried on a conversation with Mikey and Jimmy, while Kyle walked over to join them.

"What's the matter?" he asked. As he approached, he could tell that Brian looked a little pale and had sweat on his brow.

"No clue," Brian said keeping his voice steady. "Feel like I'm gonna puke."

"I thought it might be the chicken," Mikey explained. "But we all had it, too."

"I'm fine guys," Brian interjected. "I'm gonna go sit down and drink a water."

"Good call," Kyle said. "Want anything from these snacks?"

"Oh, God no, but thank you."

Brian left the group and sat down at an empty table near the restrooms in the far corner of the gym.

"He looks like shit," Jimmy said. "He should go home. Dunno why he's hanging out here."

"I agree," Kyle said. "Let me go see if my parents have left yet and they can take him."

Kyle ran through the doors to the parking lot with no idea where they would have even parked. He scanned around with no luck as he walked up and down the two rows of parked cars.

So much for trying to help a friend, he thought and started back towards the gym. A lone engine revved and roared in the silent lot with rubber screeching on concrete to join the symphonic chaos. Smoke and dust swirled in the air from the next row of cars, and he caught enough of a glimpse to see it came from a white SUV.

It's them! It's fucking them!

He couldn't see all of the vehicle to be certain, but it appeared to face the gymnasium straight on. Kyle turned his attention to the open door of the gym and could see people walking by, oblivious to the happenings outside.

The SUV, a Ford Explorer he could tell for sure now after moving a little closer, released its brake while the engine still howled. Approximately eight car lengths separated the Explorer from the gym entrance, and Kyle watched in dismay as that distance reduced in a matter of two seconds.

An exploding crunch and cracking sound echoed around the deserted parking lot as Kyle froze. Muffled shrieks escaped the gym, but the main entrance remained blocked as three quarters of the Explorer barricaded the doorway.

People started flooding out of the gym's other door further down. He noticed parts of the brick exterior had collapsed inwards from the impact, leaving a slight gap for him to see within the building. From his distance, he could only see general body figures, some covered in blood, others running frantically. He could only see adults, figuring his classmates weren't tall enough to appear through the gap in the exterior.

The brake lights flickered on the rear of the Explorer sticking out of the building while smoke from the engine poured out of the doorway as the engine fell silent.

Mr. Romano sprinted out of the building, his bald head smeared with blood. He ran to the other end of the parking lot and disappeared behind a couple of cars.

Knowing his friends were inside, possibly injured, Kyle broke towards the cafeteria doors around the side of the school while the parking lot filled with parents and students alike, with cell phones in hand, calling for ambulances.

The cafeteria, to his surprise, was deserted. There was nothing left in there but a few unattended trays from the lunch that had been served. He could see a handful of people hiding in the kitchen behind the cafeteria's main dining area. No one he recognized, however.

The cafeteria connected to the gym via a sliding door. When he pulled the door aside, the first thing he saw was the front of the Explorer, which looked nothing like a car anymore. It reminded him of the times he used to stomp on soda cans for the recycle bin.

The smoke fogged up the gym with an effect similar to the fog machines employed within haunted houses. The stench of burnt rubber mixed with vomit rushed his senses, causing him to use every ounce of composure he had to keep from contributing to the odor.

From the inside, the hole in the wall appeared much larger. Brick and concrete splattered across the furthest depths of the gym floor, and a thick crack ran its way from above the blood-splattered SUV to the ceiling, letting some of the sunlight shine through.

Kyle's gaze dropped to the front of the unrecognizable vehicle where a pool of oil and antifreeze mixed with the deep red of blood to surround three bodies on the ground in what looked like a pool of grape juice. He recognized one as Mr. Swirsky, and another as Emily Marsh, a girl from his English and Science classes.

Mr. Swirsky's arm shivered beyond his control as he blinked his eyes in a rapid succession to keep blood from getting into them. Both of his legs snapped midway up his thigh and bent in opposite directions to form a letter T with his body.

Ms. Ortiz darted across the gym to help the three lying on the floor. Their blood spread out far from the vehicle, causing her to slip and fall on her bottom. She gasped as some of the gore splashed onto her face.

Emily laid still since Kyle first noticed her. Blood blanketed her face so he looked to her chest to see if it rose and fell. It did not and he assumed the worst for his classmate's fate. The third body laid face down, but Kyle did see it breathing, and even a slight wriggle of the fingers from the arm that bent the wrong way at its elbow. A splinter of bone stuck out of the person's bicep like a stick in the mud.

Across the gym, Kyle saw Brian seated at the same table from earlier, watching the chaos unfold with a rather calm demeanor on his face. This sent chills up Kyle's spine, as he no longer *seemed* like the friend he had known for years. He scanned the room for Mikey and Jimmy, but didn't see them, figuring they had already fled.

Multiple sirens screamed as they approached; police cars screeched to a stop right outside of the gym doors as policemen and paramedics rushed to the scene inside the nearly deserted gymnasium. A handful of people were injured by flying debris from the building and hobbled around with obvious leg injuries, while others hid underneath tables and in the far corners of the room. Kyle remained in the cafeteria doorway, unable to grasp what he had just witnessed. Brian had left his spot at that the table while Kyle wasn't looking and now he couldn't find him.

Two firemen examined the totaled SUV stuck in the doorway while six others tended to the bodies sprawled out in front it. Kyle kept an eye on Emily as the medics performed CPR to try and resuscitate her. After numerous attempts the young medic pulled away, shaking his head in disappointment. The image of Emily being zipped into a body bag would forever remain with Kyle.

Mr. Swirsky and the unknown man had been strapped to stretchers. The blood was wiped away with a half-hearted effort and it still covered most of their faces. They were led out of the door side-by-side, thrust into the back of two ambulances, and driven off in seconds.

Kyle regained enough control over himself to wander outside. Dozens of his classmates and their parents were scattered across the parking lot, some being stopped for a statement from the police. He didn't recognize any of the adults, apart from some of his teachers. A helicopter chopped its blades above the school for news coverage of the incident.

Coach Ostrom provided an animated statement for the police, throwing his hands in the air with emotion. Kyle knew Mikey and Jimmy's parents attended the ceremony, but couldn't locate them in the mob of people. His pocket vibrated and he pulled out his phone to find his mom calling.

"Ky, are you okay?" she yelled in a panic before he could even say hello.

"Yes," he said in a shocked tone. "I was outside when it all happened. I watched it all. I didn't know the car was gonna do *that!*"

"Oh, thank God! Your friends just got here and told us what happened. Their parents are headed back to the school to see if anyone needs help. They were worried when they couldn't find you."

Kyle's relief settled in, untwisting some of the knot in his stomach that had formed. "Oh, good, I've been looking for them here. Is Brian there too?"

"Yes, he showed up a little after everyone else. I know Lori was at work today, so I called her to let her know."

Her tone sounded normal, meaning Brian couldn't have still had that ghastly look on his face. "Okay, I'm coming home then. I can't watch this anymore," Kyle said and hung up. The timing still didn't make sense from when he saw Brian at the table to receiving the call, but he figured one's sense of time could be thrown off course after such a traumatic event.

Kyle raced home, leaving his school in a state of disaster never experienced before, and knowing he couldn't leave a statement with the police because of the gray man theory. He suspected something much bigger was taking place, but couldn't pinpoint exactly what.

12

"No way!" Susan cried to herself from her office. She had fled the school right after the SUV crashed, and had received an email minutes before from Colonel Griffins, warning her that the Exalls were in the area. Her ETD confirmed this.

The handheld ETD devices were no bigger than a typical cell phone, and came equipped with the same advanced capabilities that the master devices had at headquarters. Red dots on the map represented Exalls, and green dots showed her fellow humans. When she checked her ETD at the school, a red dot flashed right outside of the building, somewhere in the parking lot. Once she stepped outside, she saw Kyle hiding and knew as long as he was safe, she could justify running home to strategize her next move.

The Exall attack was supposed to occur on Saturday, not Friday, according to their intel. The surprise caught the entire department off guard and word made it back to the White House where the President declared a private State of Emergency, enabling the Crew to utilize any means necessary for the protection of citizens.

Susan had never experienced this order and felt excited at the thought of it because keeping things new and fresh had that effect. She could officially ignore policies and procedures to kill the Exalls, so if she wanted to barge into a room and start shooting like Scarface, then she would.

In her office, fear settled in as she saw numerous red dots on the ETD scattered across her own neighborhood. From what she had heard on the news, no one at the school questioned the fact that the Explorer lacked a driver. Shock could leave people scatterbrained, but she suspected the Exalls influenced the minds of those people to overlook that major detail. In fact, two Exalls still roamed the school grounds, likely blending in with all the commotion to admire their work.

A lone red dot sat in front of Travis and Lori's house and she knew the time had come.

During the previous attack many years ago, Susan had wiped out an entire family of Exalls, six in total, as part of an ambush. One of those six managed to survive and escape, but made sure to tell Susan he would "never forget, and one day you'll be sorry."

These words often caused the nightmares she experienced. His black eyes peered through her soul in those dreams. She could feel the daring tickle of death in that stare. The stench of the dead corpses came back in the dreams too. The smell of their black blood oozing was like rotten eggs.

Exall bodies decayed instantly and could dissolve into a dust matter within four hours. At the time, this fact was a lesson learned as no one had previously killed an Exall. New procedures were enforced with hopes of preserving an Exall corpse for further studies.

But I don't need to follow those today, she thought. Survival and murder weighed on her mind. Oftentimes, only a fine line could separate the two.

She did plan on returning a body, however, and bonus points if it could be from the same bastard who threatened her family.

The Crew had a way of being either a rewarding or thankless job. Moments like these she would put in the rewarding column.

"I'm gonna kill him," Susan said while she slung a carrying case with her assault rifle over her shoulder. She checked the ETD to find the red dot now inside of her son's home. "You picked the wrong day, you piece of shit."

She tucked the device back into her pocket and stormed out of the house on a mission. The warmth of the day graced her as she stepped down from her front porch and marched towards the sidewalk.

She felt odd to find any sort of joy in the day, but the thought of her long career with The Crew winding down to a close pleasured her. She could end her career with a figurative and literal bang. *It's a beautiful day to kill the scum,* she thought as she passed some neighbors planting their new flowers for the up coming summer.

It's a good day to die, too, another voice buried in her conscience echoed back. A tight-lipped smile helped her keep her composure. A clip of her special bullets issued by The Crew rubbed against her belly underneath an extended tee shirt.

The bullets were nicknamed "chokers" and resembled the design of a nine millimeter. The creators made them with a unique functionality to explode upon impact and release a chemical called crystalline to absorb all the oxygen from its host.

Since the Exalls lacked typical organs, such as lungs, this special ammunition became the only known way to kill one. Their bodies absorb oxygen in a similar way to how plants absorb energy from the sun to live. The crystalline in the bullets sucked all the oxygen from them, suffocating them to death.

Susan fell in love with the bullets upon their release because they did not require an accurate shot. The ammo would function anywhere it entered an Exall's body. Once the bullet sensed the dramatic temperature drop of their internal coldness, it exploded and killed the enemy within seconds.

She turned the corner and saw her son's home through a bush that hadn't quite awoken from its winter nap. The leaves on the neighbors tree ruffled in the breeze as she approached and checked her ETD, which showed four green dots inside the house with a red one in the midst of them.

If this son of a bitch hurt anyone, I'm emptying this whole clip into its head.

Based on their behavior, she knew it was unlikely the Exall had done anything. They were twisted creatures and would want Susan to watch them get their revenge. The new knowledge of their shape shifting capabilities also factored in as the Exall was probably disguised as someone she already knew.

But who?

Susan glanced at the ETD once more before entering the house. She rang the doorbell and tried to relax. The last thing she needed was questions about what she had in the bag. *Just act normal.* She needed to identify the Exall and eliminate them to ensure everyone's safety.

Travis opened the front door and, to her relief, chatter carried out from the living room.

"Hey, Mom," Travis greeted. "We're all here talking about the crash at the school. You'd left already, but did you hear about it?"

"Of course. I heard all the sirens and put on the news," she responded while scanning the living room. "Are you all okay?" Their responses blurred into her subconscious as she concentrated on who was in the room. The TV hung on the wall and played a daytime baseball game that Kyle and his friends watched from the couch.

It's one of them. Please not Kyle.

"One of our classmates died," Kyle said. "I saw it."

The boys looked around in uncomfortable silence, clearly a topic that had already been discussed multiple times but no easier to hear.

"I'm sorry to hear that, boys." Susan hated nothing more than Exalls that killed children.

She took a mental note of the order the boys sat on the couch from left to right: Jimmy, Kyle, Brian, and Mikey.

"I need to use the restroom. Please excuse me," Susan turned the corner down the hallway as her pulse raced and throbbed throughout her body, and she closed the bathroom door behind her.

"Okay, it's okay," she whispered and leaned over the sink. Her hands trembled like she had Parkinson's disease as she pulled the ETD out from her front pocket.

The screen flashed its colors of red and green on the interactive map. Four dots ran in an even line besides each other, all green except for the third one from the left.

Brian.

Susan slid the map with her thumb to get a view of Brian's house across the street. No dots of any sort within the vicinity, meaning no one was home. "This can't be," she whispered again.

The briefing she had reviewed with her team mentioned that Exalls could mirror the appearance of humans through injecting their blood into the human host. She saw Brian at the school and knew he couldn't have driven the SUV into the building because she had watched on her ETD to make sure Kyle and his friends remained as green dots; if someone were to die, they turned black.

The boy in the living room was Brian Carsner. Well, he *looked* like Brian Carsner. The truth that Susan had trouble grasping was that she would have to kill or injure him, and then figure out how to explain why to all of his friends. She needed to remain calm and in control, so she stormed out of the bathroom with big strides back into the living room.

"Sorry all, I need to step outside and make a phone call," she said as she passed them, not waiting for a response. She stepped out of the door onto the front porch and felt warmth rush upon her already flushed face. Travis sat stiff as a board in his recliner and watched her through the screen door. The boys paid no attention and kept watching the game, while Brian looked slightly pale. He had snapped at Travis when asked if he was feeling okay.

Lauren left Brian with his friends rather than at home while she went out to pick up some medicine for him. Lori joined her on the trip as everyone in town was skeptical about going out alone after the events at the school.

Susan's distorted voice could be heard from outside, but not clearly enough to make out her exact words. Travis sensed that the school event was no coincidence, and that she may have to do something about it.

"Colonel Griffins, we have a situation," she explained into her cell phone. She held her ETD in her other hand to keep an eye on things. "I believe I have one that has taken over a human completely."

"Wells," a nervous voice responded. "I know. We've had six internal cases in the past two days. People have called out sick, then showed up to work. We lost a few people. There was a shooting in the office last night."

Susan continued to listen in disbelief as Colonel Griffins explained the horrific scene at the Crew's headquarters in D.C. where a member named Jonathon Browne came into work after calling out sick and wreaked havoc on everything.

He changed the programming of the Crew's main ETD in the headquarters to not show any red dots, leaving them vulnerable to attacks from Exalls. After that, he took out his government issued pistol from his desk and shot his nearby coworkers before the Marine's on security duty shot him to death.

The surviving programmers fixed the software and revealed two Exalls within The Crew's building, mimicking the appearance of regular members. Colonel Griffins called for a quarantine of the building until they could study the two detained Exalls in their custody, a first opportunity in The Crew's history. He had started his research on the matter when Susan had called.

"Sue, are you there?" he asked after a few seconds of silence. She had fallen into a mild shock upon learning of the events.

"Yes, Sir, sorry," she finally responded. "I'm so sorry to hear all this."

"Nothing to worry about. We have it under control now," he said with a false confidence. "Now, I suggest you get back to your problems over there before anything else happens. You have my blessing to do anything you see necessary. We're in a full on war now."

"Yes, Sir, thank you. I'll follow up as soon as I can."

She ended the call and sat down on the porch, letting her arms and legs dangle over the edge. Rays of sunlight fought their way through the neighbor's tree, making Susan look down to the ground while she contemplated her next move. The world seemed to stand still in the midst of the silence. *Is this what the end of the world feels like?*

Susan had wanted to inform Colonel Griffins about the police officer that was injured earlier in the week, but the news of chaos at their headquarters derailed all of her thoughts. Whenever any non-Crew members had an encounter with Exalls, they sent someone out to check in on them and stressed the importance of not sharing any details about the beings they tangled with. The last report she heard from her team mentioned the officer was recovering at the intensive care unit at Denver General Hospital and could barely speak, but would make it.

She brushed the thoughts aside to focus on the current issue. Brian had Exall blood pumping in his veins and didn't even know it. For all he knew, he had just caught the flu or a stomach bug. She would somehow have to isolate him from the bunch before his symptoms grew worse and turned him into a mindless killing machine.

If it comes to it, I'm going to have to kill this boy I've known since he was born. The thought made her queasy, but the truth was she could no longer view him as Kyle's friend. He would try to kill her first, without second thoughts, and she couldn't afford to be caught off guard.

Susan rose from the porch and paced up and down the empty driveway since Travis parked his truck on the curb. She stopped on the sidewalk and faced Brian's house across the road. She debated calling in some of her squad members who had posted up in different parts of town for the day. She decided it would be safe and pulled out her phone to call one of them.

Before she could dial a number, a scream came from the house and Kyle burst through the front door with eyes full of fear. Mikey and Jimmy followed as they all jumped off the porch onto the front lawn.

Susan dropped her bag to the ground and unzipped it, pulling out her "thumper" that she already loaded with her special bullets. "Everyone behind me now!" she commanded the boys. Mikey and Jimmy obeyed without hesitation and lunged behind her.

Kyle stood frozen in his tracks, eyebrows raised in puzzlement at the sight of his grandmother holding an assault rifle almost as big as him. "Grandma, wha–"

"Get back NOW!" she snapped. "Where's your father?"

Her gun and eyes stayed fixed on the front door.

"Brian pulled a knife on him," Kyle explained as he crouched behind her next to his friends. "Dad kicked him off and Brian ran out the backdoor."

"Did he cut your dad? Did you see any blood?"

"No." Kyle tried to sound more together than he truly was. "He held the knife to his throat, but that's it."

"Okay, good. Let's get him and get over to my house."

Her hand trembled again as she fumbled in her pocket for the ETD. Knowing Brian's precise location was critical to their survival and the map showed his flashing red dot four houses down and moving further, towards the school. *They got him.* She could see a green dot still in the living room and shouted for Travis to come out.

He appeared in the doorway with a shotgun rested over his shoulder. Susan made sure her son remained equipped to handle any scenario that might come as a result of her profession, and while she couldn't give him any chokers, he still had the latest and greatest in weaponry.

"Ma!" he shouted as he stepped outside. "Something you've

been meaning to tell me?"

"We need to get to my house right now. Then I'll explain."

"Okay, let's go. Everyone in my truck!" One thing Susan always made clear to Travis was that if something happened, don't ask questions and follow instructions. He also jumped off the porch and fled across the small lawn to his truck.

"Quickly, let's move!" Susan panted. The boys followed suit like a group of toddlers obeying their parents.

Susan grabbed the shotgun from Travis and sat in the passenger seat with both guns across her lap. *Riding shotgun with a shotgun,* she thought and cracked a smile.

The boys piled into the backseat as they had on the camping trip, but they had more space with Brian's unexplained absence.

Travis powered up the truck and glanced around the neighborhood to see if anyone was looking out from their homes. To his surprise no one was, and he figured they were probably at work or watching the news coverage of the attack down the street.

He could get to his mom's house in one minute exactly under normal circumstances, but today he had thirty seconds on his mind as he released the parking brake and jerked the truck forward. Susan started to explain.

"I can't give you boys too many details for your own good. There are people here to hurt us. They took control of Brian, so don't think your friend is the one who pulled out a knife. These people are dangerous. I have a panic room at home where we can all be safe." They all stared at Susan, wheels cranking around in their head to grasp everything.

"Grandma, what is all this?" Kyle asked. "Why do you have a gun and know these things?"

"I can't go into that now. We'll have a family talk once this is all over."

Her tone was firm and the conversation dropped at that point. Mikey and Jimmy, who sat on each side of Kyle, looked at him as if awaiting a response, but looked out of their windows after realizing he wouldn't push the matter any further.

Under a minute, Travis praised himself as he pulled into his childhood driveway. He may have run a couple of stop signs, but it's only illegal if you get caught, right?

"Wait a minute!" Susan barked as Travis opened his door. She needed to check her house on the ETD. She found nothing inside, but she did see three Exalls at the school two blocks parallel. One of them was Brian, she was sure of it. Emergency responders and news vans flooded the parking lot from what she could tell.

"Alright, let's go in through the backdoor and head straight down to the basement," she instructed.

Kyle craned his neck in effort to see his grandma's gadget with no success. Mikey and Jimmy jumped out of the truck, not needing to be told twice, while Travis jogged to the backdoor with Kyle and Susan following.

He jiggled the keys to unlock the door, and dashed down the stairwell that descended from the entryway. Mikey and Jimmy stood at the top of the stairs and looked down into the darkness of the basement like it was a mystic land.

"Go!" Susan shouted, losing her patience with the boys. A large painting of The Last Supper hung above the stairwell and she felt a similar fear and uncertainty to what she imagined Jesus felt that night at the dinner table.

A light flicked on in the basement, enticing Mikey to finally step down. Kyle looked back over his shoulder and gave Susan an uneasy look.

"We'll talk, Ky," she assured him. "I just need you to do as I say for now."

"Alright, I want to know everything," he said and stomped down the stairs.

Jimmy and Mikey observed the massive bookshelf that covered the entire back wall of the basement. Almanacs and encyclopedias from every decade since the fifties filled its shelves. While they gawked at the wealth of knowledge before their eyes, Travis paced in circles around the sofa set up in the middle of the basement living room.

Pictures of Kyle's grandfather decorated the walls in the living space, and he felt nostalgia start to creep in, but shook it off at once.

"I need you all to focus and snap out of it," Susan demanded. "I have a panic room down here. You'll all be safe. Lauren and Lori are still out and about. One of my team members will notify them of the situation and also keep them safe."

"Are these real aliens?" Jimmy spoke for the first time since the school banquet.

"Everything you see and hear today needs to stay with you," she continued, not acknowledging Jimmy's question. "You can't even speak to each other about this after today. For your own safety I hope we're clear."

Everyone nodded in agreement. Travis rocked back and forth, fidgeting with his fingers, while Kyle noticed his eyes dance around the room at the pictures of his late father.

"Jimmy, we don't like to use the word *alien*, but these are a different species of people; far more advanced than us and dangerous."

Jimmy's already pale face flushed out the last drops of color.

He had always loved conspiracy theories, especially those about Area 51 and Roswell, New Mexico. But hearing it come to life proved to be more than he could handle.

"No such thing," Mikey also spoke for the first time in a while. "Clearly something is going on and we're in danger, but there's no super human species. If there is, then I'll sit here and wait for Superman to come rescue me."

"Look, we can bicker over *my* life's work or you can follow me and not get killed today!" Susan did not appreciate Mikey's snide remark. She turned and stormed down the short hallway that connected the living room to the laundry room, bathroom, and her walk-in pantry.

She entered the pantry on her right and pulled down a drawstring to illuminate the pitch black room. The rest filled in behind her, cramming the space between three tall racks of dry and canned foods.

You could grocery shop down here, Mikey thought as he drooled over the boxes of macaroni and cheese stacked to the ceiling.

In the corner of the room sat a worn down, discolored chest freezer. Once white, it had faded into a dirty yellow tint after decades of use. Susan flipped open its lid, letting a gust of cold air flow across the room, and began rummaging through bags of frozen chicken and boxes of oven-bake dinners.

They had formed a semicircle around her and watched as she grunted to reach the lowest depth within the freezer. She brushed some frost away to reveal a small red button no bigger than her fingertip that hadn't been touched in almost five years; some force needed to be applied to pop the button into its socket.

She pushed then watched as the entire floor of the freezer collapsed into a momentary pit of darkness. A few seconds passed as Susan remained head first in the freezer before fluorescent lighting flickered its way to life in the panic room. The floorboard laid on the ground like a knocked out fighter, staring up at her in wonder. All she could see were a couple of chairs along the wall, but that was how the panic room had been designed, to minimize visibility from above.

"Okay, Jimmy," she said after raising her head out of the freezer with frost clung to the top of her head. "You're the tallest one here so you'll have the shortest drop down. About five feet if you hang from the freezer."

Jimmy shot her a doubtful look which said, *I'm not going in there.*

"Once you land, you'll see a small ladder against the far back wall. If you set that up against this opening we can all get down easily."

Jimmy shuffled to the front of the freezer and looked down into the hole, judging the drop to be less than Susan mentioned. Everyone but Susan reciprocated his look of anxiety when he looked back up at them. Travis kept looking from his mother to the freezer. She had sent him downstairs to get food from it countless times and had never mentioned a trap door.

"Well?" Susan questioned, burning a stare in to Jimmy.

"Ok, I'll go," he said as he peered down the hole again.

"Great. Just climb in the freezer and hang onto the edge of it. Just let go when you're ready to land below." Susan remained authoritative and cold.

Jimmy did as instructed, and hoisted his body into the open freezer, clinging onto the edges like a child on monkey bars. Ice and frost from the inside wall scraped his arms, but his rush of adrenaline didn't allow him to feel it.

The concrete flooring greeted his feet with a *thump* that

echoed in the small panic room. He didn't even notice the jolt in his knees, as awe took over his senses. Some folding chairs leaned against the back wall next to the ladder he needed to retrieve, and along his right, bottles of water lined up in unison with some boxes and cans of food. The glow coming from his left caught him in a daze, however. Thirty monitors covered the length of the wall, each showing a different area of Susan's house and yard.

Jimmy's eyes darted across the screens and found the one that showed his friends standing around the freezer just above him.

"You see it?" Susan echoed from above. He looked up and saw her head poked over the opening.

"Yeah, sorry," he shouted up. "I wasn't expecting all this."

He strolled along the wall of screens to the ladder that stood as tall as him, allowing him to grab it with ease and return to the opening.

"Perfect. Extend it up to me," Susan instructed.

Jimmy leaned the ladder against the wall and extended it to its maximum length, rattling it in his hands when Susan grabbed the top end to secure against the edge of the freezer.

"Alright, gentlemen, we're ready," she told them in their tight-knit circle.

Travis stepped up first, still refusing to question any instruction, and swung his legs over the freezer to the welcome feeling of the sturdy ladder. While he lowered himself into the panic room, Susan checked her ETD to find two red dots approaching her house, still a block away, with Brian still at the school along with many others.

Kyle and Mikey remained in the pantry with Susan and watched her tuck the ETD back into her pocket with a trembling hand.

"We need to move quickly," she snapped at them. "Mikey, I need you to get your shit together now and get down there!"

The look of uncertainty left his face for the first time in hours, only to be replaced by genuine shock. As a straight A student and reliable son, he had never been yelled at before.

He obliged and lunged towards the freezer. "I'm so sorry, Mrs. Wells. I guess I still can't believe what I saw."

"I get it, but we need to hurry! We can talk later."

Mikey looked down into the freezer for the first time and saw Jimmy staring up back at him. He knew that regardless of what was going to happen, his friends would be by his side, so he hopped into the freezer and slid down the ladder without much thought.

Susan confirmed he had landed safely and could hear the three of them down there conversing as if they were at a social gathering. She took a couple steps back from the freezer and stood right in front of Kyle. Her eyes welled up with tears.

"Ky, whatever happens, just know I love you." Her lips quivered and her voice shook. "I want to tell you in case this is my only chance."

Kyle felt sick, not fighting off his tears as they poured down his face. His throat felt swollen to the point he couldn't respond.

"It'll all be fine," Susan continued. "And don't mind your dad. He's doing and acting exactly as I've been telling him for years in case this ever happened."

The web of confusion and questions continued to tangle in his mind as he felt left out of some family secret he should have known about.

"You'll understand all this when it's time," Susan said,

having gained control of her emotions. "Go down there and trust me. There's a small amount of laughing gas pumped into the room so you'll all feel more relaxed."

He lunged into his grandma's embrace and squeezed her tight, sobbing out of control.

"I love you, Grandma." His crying gave way to heavy panting. She released her arms from around his shoulders and could see his puffed red eyes. She glided her hand across his cheek to wipe away the remaining tears.

"It's time, Ky," she said.

Kyle nodded and dragged himself to the freezer. He could hear laughter but couldn't see anyone in his line of vision. Susan helped him into the opening and kissed his forehead as he secured a grip on the ladder.

"Remember, it's all going to be okay," she assured him. "Just hang tight down there until I come back to get you."

His feet hit the ground and the perky conversation in the panic room ceased. He never broke his stare from looking up until he saw his grandma close the lid of the freezer, trapping them underground for God knows how long.

Susan clasped the locks on the freezer – both the standard and the additional security ones. She stacked some boxes of cereal on top of the lid to make it look less disturbed.

From above, a sharp bang thundered into the basement. Susan grabbed her rifle that she had laid over the cans of beans on the front shelving unit.

She knew the sound and what it meant. Her backdoor had been kicked open, and she felt her palms clam with sweat.

They're here.

13

Kyle felt it within seconds of his enclosure in the panic room. His grandma told him small doses of laughing gas would relax the mood.

Either she lied about the amount or we have different meanings of "small".

The darkness above him seemed to go into eternity after she closed the lid on them. He turned to find Jimmy and his dad in the midst of a debate regarding the new baseball season for the Rockies. Mikey had pulled up a chair along the back wall and let his head glide from left to right as he observed the wall of monitors, struck by a nerdy ecstasy.

His fascination drew Kyle to look at all the black-and-white colored screens. He caught a glimpse of the screen that showed his grandma, and saw she remained in the pantry, leaning against one of the shelves with her rifle in hand.

Three monitors across, he could see the back door entryway that they had all come through moments ago. The door looked cracked down its center while the door framing lay splattered across the floor in a mix of dry wall dust and wood shards.

A man stood in the entryway, looking down the stairs to the basement. He wore black sunglasses with slicked back hair as dark as night.

The figure of another man stood behind him on the steps

outside. One of the monitors had a better angle, but only from the rear. He appeared as tall as the doorway, a good head length taller than his partner, and donned a fedora that shaded his face.

"Guys, will you pay attention?" Kyle snapped. "My grandma is in danger." Travis and Jimmy fell silent and worked their way over to some closer seats like they were sitting in a movie theater.

"I've been here a hundred times and have never seen any security cameras," Mikey said. "She has every inch of this property covered." His eyes twinkled in amazement.

"Oh shit, look!" Travis barked. It took a minute for him to see what was going on above their heads, with the numerous screens, most of which showed nothing but empty rooms of his childhood house. "We need to help her. I can't sit here and watch this."

"You can't," Mikey said. "She closed the lid and locked it in seven different places. We're not going anywhere."

His words hung in the air as they let that fact sink in, and Travis fell silent with a look of deep thought. He crossed his arms and refocused on the monitors.

For Travis, the sight of his mother kissing a small crucifix she wore around her neck built up the angst and tension within him.

There has to be a way out of here.

If his mother had taught him anything, it was that there is always a way. He only needed to find it.

* * * * *

Susan leaned back on a rack of canned soups, trying to breathe quietly to allow complete silence. She glanced at her ETD to confirm two Exalls stood at the top of the stairs.

The rifle, loaded with a full magazine of her beloved chokers, throbbed in her hands. If the Exalls wanted her they would need to come down the stairs. Descending single file would be their only option, and Susan knew that was the opportunity needed to take them on one at a time. She also knew they were aware of that fact. Nothing with the Exalls was ever as straight forward as it seemed.

She jumped from the pantry across the hall to the laundry room. She wanted to turn the lights off in the living room, but didn't want to go near the stairway where the light switch was located, knowing they would be waiting for her. The house's breaker box was hidden in the back corner of the laundry room, leaving her secluded and out of sight to peacefully cut the power to her entire home if she wished.

She stomped over a pile of laundry to make way, hands flailing towards the box in excitement. Dust swirled into the air when she swung open the box's panel door. The breakers aligned evenly in two columns of four, so she swiped them all with two quick strokes. They snapped into their *off* positions and the basement plunged into blackness.

She had no windows in the basement, leaving the only glow of light as that which shone down from the open backdoor atop the stairway. Everything else in the basement took cover under the darkness.

I could lure them down here. Nothing has ever proved they could see in the dark.

Susan had her night vision goggles in her bag and would be able to shoot them with ease.

"Oh, Susan!" a monotone voice shouted from above. She had

returned to the hallway between the laundry room and pantry, feeling her way through the dark. "You think we're going to fall for your games?"

She peeked out of the hallway and saw the stream of light shining down the stairs, reminding her of how she imagined the stairway to heaven might glow in its glory. The shadow of the Exall cut right down the middle of the stream of light.

"We're not going down there," the voice continued. "You think we waited all these years to lose a shootout in the dark."

Years? They've been studying us for as long as we've been studying them.

"Get the fuck up here, or we'll blow up your entire house including your pathetic hideout room down there!"

A clinging sound banged its way down the stairs and settled on the landing floor of the basement. Susan saw what appeared to be a can shaped object. She could see smoke oozing out of its sides slowly filling the air space of the basement.

Smoke bomb, she thought and covered her mouth and nose with an open palm. Her eyes burned and itched, welling up with tears. Blinking did nothing to soothe the fire burning on her eyeballs, and her throat started to itch, causing a dry hacking cough.

She had no choice but to vacate the basement. The boys were safe below; she needed to face the Exalls.

Thick smoke reached the hallway where she hid, leaving her with one final gasp of fresh air before the burning flames would fill her lungs.

I can't die here. Not like this.

She stormed out of the hall towards the stairs while she held her breath.

"Fuck you!" she gasped in relief as she climbed the first

couple of steps with her rifle aimed up the stairs. The top landing was vacant as if no one had stood there seconds ago.

She climbed more steps and her lungs thanked her for the first batch of fresh air. She pulled the ETD out to see where her friends had gone, but the screen flickered like a TV with a poor antenna, leaving only her face in the reflection of the blank screen.

These never *malfunction,* her mind raced. She felt the adrenaline pumping into her fingertips, making them pulse like they had their own heartbeat.

The ETDs were powered and operated through the D.C. headquarters (they didn't even have a power button to turn them on or off). The blank screen meant something bad had happened at headquarters, like the story Colonel Griffins mentioned earlier.

Aside from concerns over two thousand miles away, Susan had no way of knowing the Exalls' location, or if more were on their way. They could be in the house or they could have left. It came down to a guessing game.

Do or die time. She ran up the remaining steps to find the two Exalls standing at the island in the kitchen as casually as if they were preparing lunch. Her rifle aimed right at them, yet they didn't even flinch.

"We just want to talk," the Exall in the fedora said. Her heat sunk at the sight of him. A thin, hook-shaped scar ran up from his lip. She had left that scar when she attacked the rest of his family. He had escaped her knife attack and was never seen again, until now.

"Bullshit!" Susan barked. "You've been killing our people for decades; you never want to talk!" She felt that pulsing in her finger on the trigger.

Always try to capture before killing, rang through her mind as one of the Crew's main rules.

"You can't capture us," Sunglasses said. They saw the fear swim into her eyes and grinned at each other. "Yes, we can hear everything. Even what you don't say out loud." He giggled like a schoolgirl.

"Don't count on your team to help bail you out," Fedora smiled. "They're as dead as roadkill...in fact, they *are* roadkill." He howled like a loon and it echoed around the kitchen.

Susan didn't know what to say...or think for that matter. She tried to keep her mind empty, but that was easier said than done.

"You see, Sue," Sunglasses continued. "You and us want the same things. You want to capture us. Study us. Know where we're from and how we function. And I must say, bravo to your people. You've learned quite a bit!"

Susan heard his words, but her mind muffled them into background noise as she debated pulling the trigger to blast the bastard's head off. *Capture before killing.* She also didn't know how the other Exall would react if she shot him. It could easily become her own death sentence. Their pistols rested atop the island counter, so maybe they truly meant not to cause any problems for the time being.

"All we want is the same opportunity," Fedora picked up where Sunglasses left off. "Our species is clearly more advanced than yours, but from all the other life forms we've encountered, you humans have been the most interesting."

All life forms? Susan pondered. They had teams study the most unknown parts of outer space and had never come across any other life.

"Your people are so driven by what you call emotions," Fedora explained. "One thing our kind lacks is emotion. We do what we think is best for us as a whole. We thought we wanted to implement emotions, but found so much of it used for hate and fear on your planet that we decided it would be bad for our own."

"So you think you're the galaxy's morality police?" Susan refused to lower her rifle as these two had started to piss her off.

"Not at all," Sunglasses replied. "We have no concept of morality. But that's one of the many things we'd love to learn from you. It seems there's some good to all your rules and ethics, but at the same time it is strict and untrustworthy towards your citizens."

"You have entire groups of people who focus their days on making sure these rules are followed. Cops! The piggies!" Fedora cut in. "You have a written rule to not kill each other, but why? You people kill every day like it's a game. So why have the rule if it can't truly be enforced?"

"Cut the shit already," Susan snapped. "What does any of this have to do with me? Why do you kill our people in cold blood?" She could sense those black eyes behind the sunglasses examine her, daring her to pull the trigger.

"Don't you see we're doing the same thing as you, Sue?" Fedora asked back. "It's the same reason you kill us. You're unsure about us, so you kill us with hopes of studying us.

"Our intent when we came here was to learn more about your species. But we learned that you humans have no respect for life of any sort. You kill each other, you kill your planet, and it disgusts us to see such a thing happen. We're good people with no place to call home, and we deserve your planet because we'll treat it so much better."

"Bullshit!" Susan screamed. "You killed a little girl today!"

Their expressions remained flat and emotionless despite Susan's theatrics.

"We were about to be publicly exposed at that school. I could never allow that," Sunglasses said. "I drove that car into the building so you couldn't make a scene of us. We call the shots, and if we killed any of your family in the process, then even better. That girl was simply in the wrong place at the wrong time."

A bead of sweat trickled down Susan's brow and burned her eyeball as she tried to blink it away. Time seemed to stand still as she remained locked on to Sunglasses. A photo of Jesus Christ stared at her from above the kitchen sink behind the Exalls, appearing to glow.

Susan tightened her grip on the rifle, feeling its deadly powers flow through her hands, and pulled back on the trigger, firing the choker out of the barrel with a flash.

The Exall's head flung back like it took a punch to the face. His sunglasses shattered into pieces, revealing those devilish, black eyes staring blankly into space. The choker did its job as the lifeless body collapsed to the floor in a blob of gray flesh.

Exall blood, which looked like black tar, splattered across the kitchen. It also had the consistency of tar, so it didn't ooze and pool up like the human's liquid version.

Droplets of blood clung to the fedora and smeared across the jacket of the other Exall. One particular chunk, which looked more like gooey mucus, hung from the brim of his hat, an image that burned into Susan's mind for the rest of her life.

"You bitch!" Fedora shouted in a high-pitched tone. He snarled, revealing black teeth to match his eyes, and snatched the pistol off the counter, aiming it at Susan. "You'll never hurt one of us again, you evil bitch!" The pistol cracked into life, bursting a bullet into Susan's chest.

The vest she wore beneath her shirt absorbed the death he meant to cause, but knocked her off her feet. Her hands clutched where the bullet struck, grasping around to confirm she was indeed still alive. She panted for air, feeling the effects of having the wind knocked out of her lungs.

Breathe. Control yourself.

Susan exhaled steadily and in control then sat up to find her rifle at her feet, grabbing it as she stood.

Her shooter was gone. She didn't see or hear him leave, but she was in a state of shock. The Pope could have been cooking dinner at her stove without her realizing.

He's got to be in the house still.

She had fallen in front of the backdoor entrance and he would had to have stepped over to get out. She also noticed the front door still closed with no sign of a flustered exit.

The house dimmed as clouds grayed out the sun outside. A slight breeze through the open door ruffled her hair and swirled the stench of gunpowder around the kitchen.

She checked the ETD to find the screen still blank. *Capture before kill, my ass! I'll find him and blast his head back into orbit for all his friends to see.*

Susan's confidence built back up. It needed to. She raised her rifle straight ahead and walked cautiously into the living room. The sound of rain danced on the roof and echoed throughout the silent house. *So much for a beautiful spring day.* She planned to use the sound of the exploding water droplets to her advantage and tiptoed around the living room, making sure everything was in its place. Along the wall, faces of her family with cheesy grins stared down at her from a bookshelf. Travis and Kyle were so excited as they posed in front of St. Peter's Basilica in Vatican City the prior summer.

Hope they're enjoying the show down there. Kyle is going to have a novel full of questions for me.

A hallway conjoined the living room to the rest of the house, including her office, bedroom, and bathroom. She turned her attention down this hall and kept her finger steady on the trigger.

The bedroom door remained ajar how she always left it. A grayish glow from outside spilled a dull light into the hallway. She couldn't see into the office or bathroom as the doorways ran along opposite sides of the hallway directly across from each other. The doors stood open, but that was normal.

The rain quieted to a steady sprinkle, nearly eliminating its use as a disguise for noise. All she could hear was the sound of her heart pounding away at her ribs like a jackhammer.

Her hands turned clammy, slickening her grip on the rifle, yet she kept her pointer finger snug around the trigger.

She considered throwing her own smoke bomb down the hall, but decided against it. Exalls didn't even have lungs, so all smoke would do is cloud her own vision.

She eliminated the bedroom as a possibility for his hideout due to the position of the door. The odds he had let himself in and repositioned the door where she always kept it were slim, no matter how smart he thought he was. *Attention to details.*

Office or bathroom? she debated. That left her in a classic 50/50 scenario. She could charge into either the bedroom or bathroom and face the decision of kill or be killed. *Nothing like a coin toss for your life,* she thought as her stomach twisted into thousands of knots. *If they studied my house, they'll know the office is where I keep all my info on them. There's no reason to post up in the bathroom, unless that's what he wants me to think.*

Shit.

If the damn ETD worked, this ends now.

She started to tiptoe down the hall, avoiding the spots she knew would creak. The open doors grew bigger as she approached, heart racing.

"Come out, asshole!" she shouted, hoping for the slightest tell of his location. "Come fight me like-"

An explosion boomed throughout the house, seeming to come from every direction. Susan dropped her rifle as her hands reached for her back, just above her kidney, where a burning sensation grew. She felt as if she were being cooked from the inside out.

When she looked at her hand and saw blood smothered across her fingers, her biggest fear was confirmed and a sickening feeling settled in to her gut. She looked down to see a pool of blood forming beneath her feet, not even noticing the warm trickle of it streaming down the back of her leg.

Impossible. My suit is bulletproof. I can't be shot. Little did she know, nor did anyone in The Crew, that the Exalls had also created their own special ammunition meant to penetrate the high-tech body armor worn by Crew members.

The hallway spun around her as she lost balance and collapsed to the floor. She had just enough energy, or adrenaline, she couldn't tell which, to roll over and look behind her.

Brian stood in the living room, lowering the pistol he had just fired. Except it no longer looked much like Brian. His skin darkened into a light shade of gray, and his normally light brown hair had streaks of black running through it. Black clothes covered him from head to toe like a kid ready for an intense game of hide-and-go-seek. And his eyes. They watched her as blackness took over, giving him a lifeless stare.

Brian? she tried to speak, but his name remained trapped in her mind. He turned and walked out of sight without showing any expression or emotion. Susan thought he looked possessed; he was, for all she knew.

She tried to take a deep breath, but it felt more like a desperate gasp for air. *This is it.* Her mind raced as it tried to grasp the situation. She thought about Travis and knew he could be safe and never worry again about her safety. Kyle came into her mind, and she could see him in the future. He was dressed in military attire and looked so muscular, smiling at her. *Everyone is going to be okay. I love you all.*

The spinning hallway started to slow. She thought she heard an airplane fly overhead, but sounds began to fade out. Her body numbed all over except for the burning that continued in her back.

She rolled from her side to her back, staring at the ceiling above. Her eyes closed and she could see her husband, young again, likely in his twenties from when they had first met.

His skin glowed as he grinned and reached an open hand out to her. She smiled and reached back for it, holding on tight to never let go again.

Epilogue

"Fuck!" Travis screamed. Tears streamed down his face, dripping off of his quivering lips as he looked down at the ground, avoiding the truth held within the TV screens. "Get me the fuck out of here!" He kicked and punched the walls, sobbing as he ignored the cuts and scrapes accumulating on his clenched fists.

"Dad," Kyle said, his voice wavering. "It's over. Grandma sounded like she knew this was going to happen."

"But Brian? I'm gonna kill him when I get out of here."

"That wasn't Brian," Mikey said. "You saw the look in his eyes at your house. That may be his body, but Brian is gone."

"I know she said these aren't aliens, but I think they are," Jimmy said, not looking up from his seat. "And they took Brian. Controlled him and made him one of their own."

"I should've turned that knife on him when I had the chance," Travis said. "My mom wouldn't be lying dead above me right now!" His voice elevated with each word.

Kyle stood and walked to his dad, wrapping his arms around him in a calm embrace. "She saved us. That would've been all of us up there. She knew we could live. She's our hero." The tears poured as Kyle could no longer contain them.

"Brian!" Mikey shouted. Their old friend had reappeared on the screen along with two of his new friends. "BRIAN!" The room was sound proof, no noise inside or outside could be heard.

Brian and his new friends walked to Susan's body and they all lifted her in sync. Her arms hung to the side as they retreated out of the backdoor as they held her at their sides like pallbearers.

"Bring her back, you bastards!" Travis jumped in front of the screen that showed the backdoor. "You can't take her!"

They carried her through her backyard and disappeared through the tall, wooden fence, out of sight from the surveillance cameras. Travis dropped into his chair, burying his face in the palms of his hands.

"Why didn't she just come down here with us?" Mikey asked.

"She probably knew they would find a way in," Kyle replied. "Clearly they are smart and have some sort of powers if they were able to take control of Brian."

"She lived a double life. It's something I've known about almost my whole life," Travis explained to the boys. "She always warned us that this could happen. I didn't think it actually would. We can't speak of this, and whoever they send will make sure you all know that."

Kyle felt in control, despite being trapped. He also understood his grandmother's sacrifice better than his own father. The alternative possibilities were too dangerous. They could have hijacked her mind like Brian, and had her turn on everyone trapped in the panic room. Or worse, they could have all been slaughtered by Brian had they chosen to stay out and fight alongside Susan.

The fact that his grandmother and best friend were gone hadn't quite sunk in. Shock controlled his mind and wouldn't allow him to mourn on these facts. Those emotions would have to wait even longer as three men dressed in military uniforms barged in through the open backdoor. American flags were sewn onto their sleeves, so they all assumed they were there to rescue them.

One man studied the dead Exall in the kitchen while the other two headed downstairs to unlock the freezer. The men helped them out and guided them upstairs to meet with the third, who called himself Colonel Griffins.

"I'm so sorry for your loss," he said as he removed his hat. "Susan was a true hero, and probably the greatest to never be known." Colonel Griffins towered over the boys and Travis as they all looked up at him.

"I need to know where they took her," Travis cut in, not particularly caring for an apology.

"Unfortunately, we don't know, Mr. Wells. They took her body, but cut out her tracking chip from her back. We also have no location on them, which usually means they returned to their spacecraft and won't return for another thirty years."

Travis cried at the thought of not giving his mother a proper burial.

"Your friend Brian is gone as well," he explained to the boys. "I watched all of this scene unfold while I flew here. I thought I'd make it in time. I know it doesn't mean much now, but Susan saved a ton of lives with her life's work, and her many accomplishments will preserve even more in the future."

"So what happens now?" Kyle asked.

"Fortunately, the war is over, so your safety is no longer threatened. You'll all need to recover mentally from these last few days, and we have some of the best doctors in the world to help you process everything.

"As for us, we'll be heading back to D.C. and getting back to work. We never want to see one of our own be taken away again, so trust me when I tell you that I'll personally be studying everything I can about what happened. And I'll never give up searching for your grandmother. She was like a big sister to me."

That fact was true. Susan mentored Griffins for many years as a member of her direct squad. He learned the secrets to battling simply by training with her for hours. When the time came for her to step down from her position of power she had requested Griffins be considered for the position. A recommendation from the woman who helped keep the entire program afloat went a long way in securing his current position.

"As you can imagine -and I'm sure you know, Travis- this all needs to remain silent," Colonel Griffins said while the two other Crew members hoisted the Exall body out of the kitchen. "Once you are exposed to the Exalls you become an unofficial member of The Crew. Don't take this lightly. We will know if you speak and if other people find out, and we will trace it back to you."

Kyle had no intention of compromising his grandmother's entire life's work. He saw the looks of seriousness and terror on the faces of Mikey and Jimmy. Their pact was now set, whether they liked it or not.

A week passed and their school remained closed while it underwent repairs and heavy cleaning. The entire school attended Emily's funeral service with many students sharing some of their memories of their fallen classmate.

A service was also held for Brian after The Crew explained the truth to Lauren. Her and Lori had to stay locked up in a Crew member's hotel room after being picked up from the drug store while they were out. Hours passed before the word came down for them to leave after the attack at Susan's house.

The Crew assisted in creating a phony story about Brian being injured in the gymnasium that day and passing away from complications while in the hospital. With all the chaos and blood, no one had a good enough grasp on the situation to know any different. The boys delivered an incredible eulogy together in honor of their friend while fighting through tears.

The day after Brian's service, they all flew out to Washington D.C. The Crew had arranged a ceremony to honor Susan in the nation's capital. She would have a gravestone in Arlington National Cemetery as Colonel Griffins referred to her as a "secret, but a true pioneer for the country".

The colonel's kind words fell on deaf ears. Kyle held his father's hand as they stood at the gravestone, watching his tears fall to the grass. The Crew was generous enough to fly out everyone the family wanted to attend the ceremony.

After his eulogy, Colonel Griffins approached Kyle, pulling him aside from the rest of the crowd.

"Your grandmother was an incredible woman," he said. "She also thought highly of you."

Kyle looked up at him, emotionally numb. "Thank you, sir."

"I want you to have this," Colonel Griffins pulled out a cell phone sized object wrapped loosely in a black cloth. "It was your grandmother's. It was left behind when we were going through the house. We'll be in touch when the time comes."

The colonel walked away, giving his condolences to other family members. Kyle unwrapped the cloth and looked down at the handheld device flashing green and red dots on the map on the screen. The green dots were labeled with his family members' names, himself included. He zoomed out of the map and saw numerous flashing red dots. Chills ran up his spine, so he wrapped it back up and stuffed the ETD into his pocket.

Kyle looked around at all the friends and family gathered,

wondering what secrets they all carried. He saw Mikey and Jimmy and remembered the hell they had all experienced together, and missed Brian, wondering where he was and if he even knew what was happening.

Travis sobbed next to him. Kyle knew his dad had a difficult road to recovery ahead. He had barely come to terms with his father's death and now he had to deal with the traumatic loss and kidnapping of his mother.

The worst part, he knew, was not being able to speak of what they had all witnessed that night thanks to the constant threats of The Crew. Everyone has their secrets and sometimes those secrets burdened them forever.

Thank you

Thank you for taking the time to read my work. As an independent author, receiving reviews are critical to any future success. If you enjoyed the book (or even if you didn't), I ask you to please leave it a review. You can leave reviews on Amazon, Barnes & Noble, or Goodreads, regardless of where you purchased the book. This will help me not only with promoting this current work, but future books as well. I appreciate you taking the time if you choose to do so!

I also look forward to connecting with my readers to discuss this book, or any book, for that matter. If you have not done so already, feel free to follow me on my social media sites and subscribe to my mailing list through my website!

www.andregonzalez.net
Facebook: www.facebook.com/AndreGonzalezAuthor
Twitter: @monitoo408
Instagram: @monitoo408
Goodreads: www.goodreads.com/AndreGonzalez

I'm always open to any discussion surrounding my work and would love to hear your thoughts!

Acknowledgements

One thing I learned throughout this process of self-publishing is that producing a book takes a team. I'd like to first thank my cover designer, Dane Low, for putting a face to my story. He didn't even read this book and somehow captured the essence of it based on the synopsis. My editor, Keidi Keating, for cleaning up the book to make it sound professional. This book would not be a smooth read without her touch. My aunties Chris, Tanya, and Mer for giving great feedback on making the story more complete. They helped me tie up loose ends and pointed out things I had overlooked. To all the readers, thank you for reminding me why I am doing this and keeping my fire burning to keep on going. Last but not least, my wife, Natasha, not only for her live input while reading the book next to me, but for inspiring me to finish this after all these years. This wouldn't be complete without her encouragement and support. Thank you to everyone involved, I'll see you on the next book!

Andre Gonzalez
September 6, 2016

About the Author

Born in Denver, CO, Andre Gonzalez has always had a fascination with horror and the supernatural starting at a young age. He spent many nights wide-eyed and awake, his mind racing with the many images of terror he witnessed in books and movies. Ideas of his own morphed out of movies like *Halloween* and books such as *Pet Sematary,* by Stephen King. These thoughts eventually made their way to paper, as he always wrote dark stories for school assignments or just for fun. *Followed Home* is his debut novel based off of a terrifying dream he had many years ago at the age of 12. His reading and writing of horror stories evolved into a pursuit of a career as an author, where Andre hopes to keep others awake at night with his frightening tales. The world we live in today is filled with horror stories, and he looks forward to capturing the raw emotion of these events, twisting them into new tales, and preserving a legacy in between the crisp bindings of novels.

Andre graduated from Metropolitan State University of Denver with a degree in business in 2011. During his free time, he enjoys baseball, poker, golf, and traveling the world with his family. He believes that seeing the world is the only true way to stretch the imagination by experiencing new cultures and meeting new people.

Andre still lives in Denver with his wife, Natasha, his daughter, Arielle, and is expecting a baby boy Fall of 2016.

CPSIA information can be obtained at www.ICGtesting.com
Printed in the USA
LVOW07s1145220916

505751LV00001B/1/P